Anomaly
Legacy War Book 7

John Walker

DISCLAIMER

This is a work of fiction. Names, characters, business, places, events, and incidents are either the products of the author's imagination or used in a fictitious manner. Any resemblance to actual persons, living or dead, or actual events is purely coincidental. This story contains explicit language and violence.

Blurb

One final Orb remains at large in the wild and the Gnosis
is dispatched to get it. Lost somewhere in a space station
on the edge of civilized space, early intelligence reports
suggested it would be a milk run...until a team of Pahxin
technicians went missing there. Altering their mission
parameters to include rescue, they load up an extra team
of marines and head off on the mission.

Meanwhile, back on Earth, AIA operative Christina
Dawson closes in on the traitor selling out humanity to
the Tol'An. Her people have located an old military base
currently occupied by the mercenary group responsible
for attacking Gamma Alpha. She gathers a former marine
and newly appointed AIA agent to investigate in person.

Prologue

Screams echoed off the metal walls, hordes of people reduced to little more than animal instinct. They never seemed to stop, just when one person reached the limit of their lung capacity, another took their place with just as much wild zeal. Footsteps pounded the grated floors and the high pitch clang of hollow pipes competed with the cacophony.

Zahl Dray sat on the floor of the station control room, sweat threatening to drip into his eyes. Every part of his body shook, muscle tremors from fear and strain. He struggled to breathe, to stop himself from hyperventilating. If he passed out, he would die. That much remained certain in his mind.
He brandished his sidearm, holding it in both hands. It swayed in front of him, blurring before his eyes as he stared at the only door leading into the room. He'd lost his rifle somewhere in the hallway, at least a hundred yards from where he sat. Something startled him as he ran and his hand twitched, letting the weapon fall.

A fleeting thought warned him to pick it up but before he even considered it, he was a good ten paces away. If his crew pursued him, if his former friends remained close behind, he would've been caught. The weapon would not have helped. So he was relegated to a pistol carrying eight shots.

Eight measly rounds stood between him and a gruesome murder. Much as he wanted to cling to hope, to believe he might escape his situation, his heart began to accept his fate. There were dozens of them out there, friends turned to savages and nothing seemed to scare them, not pain, not mutilation . . . not even death.

When they came for him, and they would soon, the first one through the door wouldn't even think twice about the weapon in his hand, the threat of being shot in the face. They'd die, and the person behind them would do the exact same thing. If he proved to have incredible aim, if he pulled off eight headshots, the ninth, tenth and eleventh would've torn him apart.

Zahl saw it happen to some of his colleagues before they fell prey to whatever afflicted the previous occupants. Scans indicated a tech crew from the Pahxin government, noncombatants sent to recover the station and bring it back online. Zahl's captain called them easy pickings, a quick payday.

He thought back to the moment without screams, without murder and violent death. They arrived in the system, down on their luck from two failed jobs. Hitting the station was supposed to be an easy score. Even if it had been abandoned, they could scrap the consoles, take the metal and push it off on prospectors.

When they arrived, they were surprised to find a perfectly intact and functional starship docked there. It was lightly armed, marked as one of the Pahxin government recovery units. They were essentially civilians, men and women putting their lives on the line to do humanitarian work.

Yet, Zahl's captain fully intended to take their ship and strand them there. They'd get help eventually but that score . . . A government ship would set them up for a long time. It would more than make up for the past failures, their bad luck. All they had to do was dock and make it happen.

Zahl pulled out his tablet, marveling at the fact it survived the encounter. He engaged the recorder. He figured he didn't have much time, so he wanted to put it to good use. Maybe the next people who showed up could be spared what he experienced. If he told his story, if they found it before they too were killed, then just maybe he'd die having done something right.

"My name is Zahl Dray, and I'm a pirate." He kept his voice down, speaking softly though it probably didn't matter. Those who were after him changed when their blood was up. They stopped listening, stopped speaking. The hunt and the kill became all they cared about. "Everyone needs to know what happened to my crew."

Another scream interrupted him. He closed his eyes and continued to speak. "Before I go on, take this recording and leave. Do not come here. Whatever has happened, you want no part of it. I can't even say whether I'm lucky to be alive or not. As I wait here to die, I'm thinking back on the moment we figured out how much trouble we were in."

***

Earlier

Zahl didn't want to go to the station. He would've preferred to remain onboard the ship running diagnostics. Considering how little he knew about the mechanics of their vessel, that said a great deal. Unfortunately, the captain considered him one of the better shots among the crew.

Great to be good, I guess. Zahl took up the rear while his companions took the lead. He turned to watch the airlock doors close, wondering how long it would be before they returned. While the captain convinced them all it would be an easy job, there was a complication: scans didn't show how many life signs were aboard.

That seemed like a good indication they should do some more recon. But their ship wasn't exactly outfitted with the best equipment. As long as they found valuables, they usually didn't care about anything else. Such reckless behavior worked in normal circumstances when the situation was straightforward.

But in the face of the unknown, something the pirates rarely dealt with, it became extremely dangerous. After all, they had limited resources. Even food was a luxury at times. Zahl understood their desperation this time but he would've preferred an easy raid to some poorly guarded colony.

Then at least we'd know the odds. Those colonists wouldn't stand a chance.

Neither would the technicians. When they found them.

Five of them boarded the station. Captain Rand took point. Behind him, Vorn and Qil were there to pilot their stolen vessel. Zahl and Xord were there as muscle in the unlikely event the techs had guns . . . or put up a fight at all. Chances were good they wouldn't be needed and yet, Zahl couldn't shake his nerves.

The station in question didn't register on their database. That didn't mean too much considering how long it had been since they received a proper update, but Rand seemed to think it was special. The government may have set it up to do some kind of secret research but Vorn suggested it might not have been of Pahxin design.

"What're you saying?" Zahl asked. "That this place was built by aliens? Come on."

"It's close," Vorn replied, "but there's something weird about the walls. They're just . . . I don't know . . . off."

The tech ship they planned to steal was on the opposite side of where they docked. They had few choices of where to enter. Some parts of the station didn't even have oxygen due to hull damage. That meant a good trek through the place. Zahl felt leery of his surroundings at first but after five empty modules, he dropped his guard.

"Anything on scans yet?" Rand asked.

"Negative," Vorn replied. "I can't even get through the doors as we approach them. I thought it was just proximity when we were on the ship but now, I'm suspecting interference. Someone's intentionally jamming us maybe. Or the power core in this place is emanating so much radiation, we can't get through it. Either way, this is weird."

"We know which way we're going, right?" Xord asked. "We're going the right way?"

"Yes," Rand said. "Don't worry about that. Can we raise the ship?"

"Communications remain unaffected." Vorn sighed. "How would this *only* impact scans?"

"We can ask the techies," Xord said. "When we find them."

"Just before we strand them here," Rand replied. "Though even I'm starting to think that might be a little harsh."

"This place is eerie," Qil added. "I thought it might've just been stripped down but I'm getting another feeling now. You think something happened? Something tragic?"

"Maybe," Rand said, "but who cares? That had to be a long time ago. I don't hear weapons fire and no one's even around. I'm pretty sure we're in the clear. Hell, maybe we'll get lucky and the tech crew will have already died out here. As long as we hurry and don't get caught up in this drama, we'll be perfectly fine."

The next module put them seven away from the ship they were after. Zahl checked his chronometer. They'd been onboard the station for less than half an hour but it felt longer. Even his stomach complained, acting like he hadn't eaten in days. He looked at the others, checking their expressions.

None of them showed outward signs of agitation. Zahl wondered if he was the only one feeling off. He thought to ask but Xord would've just given him a hard time. Something could've been off with the oxygen. They weren't wearing any protection because Vorn made it clear they were perfectly safe.

Zahl ran his own scan of their environment but there didn't seem to be anything off about it. He chalked it up to the unnerving quiet in the place. A power generator should've caused deck vibration, some kind of resonance but there was nothing at all. Their footsteps made the only sound and they echoed eerily down the halls.

"You know, we might be walking into an ambush," Zahl said. "Anyone on this thing can hear us coming."

"That's a good point," Rand said. "Let's slow this down. Xord, you get up here. Take point. Shoot anything that moves. We don't need to let anyone live through this."

Before Xord could make it, someone shouted to their left, a husky cry that seemed to come from the person's gut. It was answered by another directly in front of them, maybe two modules away. Rand turned, seemingly in slow motion. He was on the verge of saying something when the telltale buzz of beam weapons cut him off.

"Retreat!" Rand shouted. "God knows how many there are!"

They started running, heading back toward the ship. Heavy footfalls sounded behind them, dozens of people falling into pursuit. Xord fired behind him a couple times but Zahl had no idea what he might be aiming for. There was no sign of anyone, no indication of what they were dealing with.

Rand got on the com. "We need reinforcements!" He shouted. "Get off the ship and into position! We're leading them back to your position now!"

Vorn fell down. No one bothered to help him. Zahl glanced back, watching the man struggle to rise. Hands grabbed his legs, coming out of the shadows. They dragged him off and he cried out, screaming for aid. Zahl kept running. The thought of helping his fellow crew member didn't even cross his mind. Blind fear pushed him on.

The com lit up. Their reinforcements had boarded the station and were ready for action. "Good!" Rand shouted. "We're going to take this place by force if that's what they want."

More beam weapons cut through the air. Xord dropped to the ground. A glance showed that he'd taken a blast straight to the head. He died instantly. But there were plenty of pirates just down the hall, forty men who could back them up providing they arrived before being slaughtered themselves. Zahl fired backward several times, hoping it would slow down their pursuers. All his negative feelings, his worry, and fear caught up to him. He'd been right. The gut feeling telling him something was off had been right. If they survived, he'd pull an *I told you so* to Rand but until then, all he wanted to do was live.

Another look afforded him a good view of their attackers. The first two he saw wore metal plates on their chests. Torn pants offered a minimal amount of modesty. Their heads were all shaved and some of their faces were smeared with blood. Bulging muscles made it clear these were *not* government technicians.

What the hell did we stumble on? Zahl shot one in the face, dropping him to the ground. The man's companions hopped over the body, continuing their pursuit. Not one of them even spared their fallen a glance. Their dedication to pursuit overwhelmed their compassion for one of their own. *This is insane!*

Suddenly, the extra manpower they were rushing toward didn't seem like such a dramatic advantage. Zahl only hoped the firing line would prove enough to tear through these wild men. They were like barbarians out of some distant past, a cadre of maniacs bent on murder and mayhem.

At least the pirates only wanted money. Killing was secondary, and only when their targets resisted. These people didn't even put out a warning. They immediately escalated to deadly force and they weren't slowing down.

"We're almost there!" Rand cried. "Push yourselves, men! When you see our people, hit the deck to clear their line of fire! We'll crawl the rest of the way!"

Zahl ran until his chest felt like it might burst. He threw himself through the air, his elbows and knees slamming into the grated deck. Pain lanced through him but he ignored it, crawling forward. Their people started shooting. More screams filled the air. It became obvious they'd be hearing that for a while.

The survival of Zahl and his crew rested firmly on their ability to drive back the marauders charging their position. The battle begun, the stakes had never been higher and as the gunfire intensified, it became clear many of them would never make it off that station. Whatever malady befell the station had claimed the pirates as well.

Chapter 1

Captain Desmond Bradford stepped off the elevator onto the bridge of the Gnosis, pausing to take in the scene. After their last mission, he wanted to give Lieutenant Deacon Neville a chance to return them to Earth, providing some much-needed experience with hyperspace. Lieutenant Commander Zachary Caplan stood nearby, observing nervously.

"Relax," Desmond said as he took his seat. "I'm sure Deacon's spent plenty of time studying the workings of our helm. What're the chances of him blowing us up?"

Lieutenant Salina Gold turned from her station to answer. "Roughly sixty-three percent." They all turned eyes on her. "What? Oh, my figures come from relative inexperience combined with damage received during the mission and the random chance that we've discovered when speaking with the Pahxin about the process in general."

"Still sounds a little high," Zach said.

"Well." Salina shrugged. "Perhaps. Consider it an estimate."

"I'll consider it unnecessary," Desmond said. "If you have hard data to back that up, please keep it to yourself. I'm not interested."

"Nor me!" Deacon added. "Oh, we're getting close. Ten minutes maximum."

"Excellent." Desmond turned to his own computer, looking for a report on other personnel. Commander Vincent Bowman dropped him a line stating he was in engineering and would be on the bridge just before they emerged from hyperspace. Apparently, he was assisting Agent Cassandra Alexander and Chief Nathaniel Webber with an experiment.

Desmond checked the log to see what they were up to. It involved shield calibration on a theoretical level, computer simulations to cycle their defenses swiftly enough to counter attacks efficiently. They'd all been talking about it, but someone must've had an epiphany. The test had been going on for the better part of two hours.

The Orb they recovered remained locked up, off limits to all but senior staff. Much as it aided them to mess with the one they had before, Desmond didn't feel like taking any risks with staff while they returned this time. There was still one more out there that they knew of and he preferred to go after the sure thing rather than perform experiments.

Especially considering the one they just found had been hidden underground for an indeterminate period of time. Their own had been in the same boat and it took them some time to unlock its secrets. More importantly, this new one might not be fully functional. Attempting to tap into it without controlled conditions could be catastrophic.

They already knew the Orbs held incredible power, easily enough to destroy the Gnosis with the wrong move.

I'm probably just being paranoid, but this trip isn't long enough to pull meaningful data anyway. Besides, they had their mission ahead of them. Get the final Orb and take care of the Tol'An. Simple, clean and above all, direct. Desmond had to admit, though he signed up for exploration and science, he had been a soldier for far longer.

That wasn't to say he wanted war. He'd had enough action with the conflicts on Earth. Turning to space seemed like a quiet getaway by comparison. But when the Tol'An attacked the first time, he knew nothing would be the same again. As they encountered more of the galactic players, the universe both grew and shrunk.

Their first forays into space came at a time they thought imagined being alone. As bleak as the thought might've been, it just might've been true. No contact from any alien race in so much time then, just as they take to the stars, they were attacked. The coincidence was not lost on Desmond.

Some talked about destiny, a sense of fate driving such factors. Others suggested the activity above their planet attracted notice. Had they not taken to the stars, perhaps the Tol'An never would've found the Orb in the first place. That seemed doubtful but possible. Was the device hiding itself until the people who held it might defend it?

Maybe. So much about the devices remained unknown, even to the Pahxin. They had theirs for far longer, studying it with dozens if not hundreds of experts. Still, they found themselves unable to explain a great deal about it. Desmond found that fascinating, but another theory made the most sense to him.

Thayne Ridala, a Pahxin scientist the Gnosis saved on their first mission, suggested that the Orb unlocked information as the race controlling it became 'worthy' of the information. In other words, it held back until the people holding it would understand the knowledge they were about to possess.

"Two minutes," Deacon announced. "Be there soon, sir."

The elevator opened. Vincent stepped in, taking his seat. "Almost missed it," he muttered. "Sorry about that. They needed help with the combat simulation part of their little experiment."

"Did it seem like it'll help?"

"We'll know when they've analyzed the data." Vincent shrugged. "Looked like a lot of math to me, the kind I couldn't interpret."

Desmond smirked. "I can't wait to see the report for it. That'll be fun."

"Thirty seconds." Deacon finally sounded nervous. Simulations could do only so much when it came to preparing for the real thing. He performed the countdown, hands poised on the controls. Tapping at the last two points, the ship vibrated for a brief moment before emerging from hyperspace. "Done!"

Desmond chuckled. "Position?"

Salina answered, "right on target, sir. Perfect re-entry. Four hours to Earth orbit."

"Fantastic job, my friend," Desmond said. "Well done."

"I knew you could do it," Zach added.

"I'm not sure that's true," Deacon replied, "but I appreciate it just the same! Course heading, sir?"

"Get us home, Lieutenant." Desmond stood. "I'll be in my quarters, reporting in to Admiral Reach. Vincent, you have the bridge." He boarded the elevator just as Cassie was coming out. They nearly collided. "Sorry about that."

"It's fine." Cassie cleared her throat and moved past him. "Going for the briefing?"

"Indeed," Desmond replied. "Try not to blow anything up while I'm gone, huh?"

"I'll do my best."

The doors closed and Desmond turned to his tablet, checking the time on Earth. It should've been around four in the morning at Gamma Alpha. Admiral Reach may have been awake but he kind of doubted it. Depending on the days they were running, he'd probably be waking the man up shortly.

Back in his office, he sent the call and turned his chair, staring out the window at open space. The peace lasted less than two minutes before the com connected. Desmond turned to his screen, surprised to see Christina Dawson looking at him. He didn't think she acted as the Admiral's aide anymore after her allegiance to Intelligence came out.

Yet she'd taken his call.

"Good morning, Captain," Christina said. "I'm glad to see you made it back in one piece. I'm hoping you've got some fantastic news for us."

"I have the Orb," Desmond replied. "I was contacting the admiral to give him a quick briefing. Is he not available?"

"Emergency meeting," Christina replied. "With Dulain. It's part of the investigation into the attack on Gamma Alpha. We've got some leads and need some military support to follow them. Hence the chat with the admiral."

"Understood. I'm thinking when we arrive, we should do our best to get the Orb down there with the minimal amount of fuss. Maybe even send a couple shuttles to collect resources to establish a cadence. When the Orb gets there, security forces can show up at that point and escort it in."

"Gamma Alpha is already under heavy lockdown," Christina said. "We've got more soldiers here than some military bases, I swear. That's an exaggeration but only barely. There's also plenty of air support. Bring the Orb down in the first shuttle. I guarantee it's going to land without incident."

"Alright, that sounds good." Desmond stood. "I'm going to organize the movement of the device and get everything ready up here. We'll be in touch when we're closer. Oh . . . can you please have Admiral Reach contact me as soon as he's available? I'd like to give him some details of what we experienced out there."

"I'll be sure to put it on his calendar as soon as he's done with Dulain," Christina said. "Dawson out."

Desmond leaned back in his chair, scowling at the screen for a moment. He didn't entirely trust the intelligence division, but he knew his commanding officer needed to be more open minded. To be fair, Dulain proved to be extremely helpful when he was on board the Gnosis assisting them.

Perhaps they chose to become more of an open book. Desmond had heard they were working with Pahxin intelligence, which meant they were branching out. Their own level of paranoia wasn't standing in the way of getting work done. That was a change of pace, and it would likely benefit all parties.

Desmond tapped the com, connecting with Bowman. "Vincent, we have to get the Orb ready for departure. They've locked down Gamma Alpha hard, so we should have no trouble getting it there and stored. I'd like you to coordinate with the technicians and have them move it right away."

"Understood," Vincent replied, "anything special about it? You want marines on the shuttle with it?"

"I think that would be a good idea. Put the men on there who need some downtime. They can take shore leave as soon as they arrive and the device is locked up. Make sure Heathrow's part of that crew, will you? He definitely needs a break. Maybe even some extended time off on the planet."

"I'll talk to Fielding about it too. I'll talk to you later."

Desmond clicked off the com, glancing at his bed. He had a few hours to kill and nothing specific he needed to do. A quick nap would do him some good. He changed his status to downtime to ensure he only would be disturbed for absolute emergencies and settled in for a little rest.

When they arrived on Earth, he'd be pulled a million directions, by the doctors and administration staff. While it would be nice to sleep without a low-level vibration each evening, he knew there'd be plenty of stress to make such evenings far from comfortable. Their next action involved securing a distinct advantage against the Tol'An.

No one would be interested in remaining calm in light of that promised outcome.

***

Christina waited for Dulain outside the meeting room. The moment the door opened, she slipped in. Military people departed the room, field commanders mostly. They'd been called upon to protect Gamma Alpha in the event of another attack but the opportunity for retaliation might be close at hand.

Getting them involved seemed premature considering the small amount of data Christina and her people managed to pull thus far. Even the prisoners seemed conditioned against traditional and enhanced interrogation techniques. More time was needed before they should muster any sort of attack force.

Reach and Dulain looked up at her as she closed the door. "Good morning, gentlemen," she said. "I've come with some information that both of you might be excited to hear. The Gnosis has returned, and she's got the Orb with her."

"Thank God." Reach let out a sigh of relief. "I'm glad to hear it. How bad was it?"

"I'm not sure," Christina replied. "Desmond stated he'll tell you about the operation when he gets some face to face time. He was pretty surprised to see me answering your private com. In any event, may I ask what this meeting pertained to? I hope my assumptions are wrong."

Dulain fielded the question, "we're putting the military on alert status so they can be ready at a moment's notice. When you confirm our target, they need to be on hand to crash down upon them. It's no different than how we handled that incident in Sydney, remember? The hostage situation?"

"Improper intel," Christina explained, "could lead to a serious problem. I want to confirm anything before we turn the dogs of war loose. Do we all agree upon that at the very least?"

"Of course," Reach said. "But we do need to be prepared. These people hit us without a moment's notice. That was pretty incredible considering our security. My superiors are determined to make sure that doesn't happen again not just with defenses, but in offense as well. Whoever is doing this has to be made combat ineffective as soon as possible."

Dulain added, "Admiral, I think you have another appointment now, don't you? I'd like to have a word with Christina about the investigation in private."

"Of course." Reach stood. "Thank you both for your efforts. We'll catch up later, Dulain."

Christina watched the admiral leave before glaring at Dulain. "What exactly are you up to with him?"

"We've developed a stronger relationship now that we've had threats coming out of the woodwork. He's more receptive to my advice than ever before and all it really took was being honest. Who would've thought that?" Dulain shrugged. "And I thought for sure when he discovered you, things would step back."

"No, he can't hold a grudge for long," Christina replied. "But this military thing makes me nervous, Dulain. We're having a hard time tracking down clues on this. Operatives are pouring over data but none of it's panning out. I need more time . . . which I won't have if a bunch of military guys rattle their sabers."

"Don't worry about them," Dulain said. "They needed some assurance that they'll be involved when we take down the enemy. I'm pretty sure you and I have no interest in kicking down a door, so I figure they should hear it straight from me. We will allow them to conduct the operation when we have the intelligence to warrant it."

"And you're sure that's all you said?"

"I let them know it's our top priority as well." Dulain shrugged. "They might've read into that but none of them said so. I made no promises as to when they'd be able to take the fight to the streets as it were."

"Okay. Do you have any ideas?"

"What do we have right now?"

"One of the tech crews here caught a signal directed at some old base in Eastern Europe. Marines from Gamma Alpha took it out just before the Gnosis hyperdrive experiment. We ran a scan from satellites but didn't turn anything up but there might be activity there, even if we're not seeing it."

"Chances that's true?"

Christina shrugged. "If they're somehow involved with the Tol'An? Good. They might have the technology to do it. But I don't personally think they're directly related to the enemy. Or at least, not in contact with them. I think they've been given coordinates to send things but that they have a different contact. A Pahxin likely."

"Scary, but plausible." Dulain hummed. "I think we need to get you out there."

"Get me out there?" Christina shook her head. "I'm the lead on this case, not the field operative."

"You're the best person we have for this type of thing right now," Dulain said. "Don't go alone, of course, but get out there and do some recon. If you find that there is activity, give the military their attack. It'll be the first, I'm sure because that won't be the whole story. At least, I doubt it will."

"I hate Eastern Europe," Christina muttered. "It's cold as hell over there this time of year."

"And that base you're referring to is in the mountains if I'm not mistaken," Dulain pointed out. "Definitely going to be an uncomfortable experience. Just make it quick. If you're fast, you'll be in and out of there before you know it. If it's empty, then maybe there's some residual evidence, something leading us to the next clue."

"I know how it works." Christina sighed. "Alright, I'll prep for the op right now. I told Bradford to bring the Orb down in their first shuttle. He'll coordinate with security when he arrives I'm sure."

"Thanks. The sooner it's locked up the better." Dulain stood. "We'll talk when you get back. Be safe out there and don't do anything too crazy. I can't afford to lose you."

"That might just be the nicest thing you've ever said to me," Christina replied. "I feel like I should . . . ask for a raise or something."

Dulain grinned. "I *might* afford to lose you at that point."

"Hilarious." Christina chuckled. "Okay. Bye for now." She left, heading down to her quarters. Along the way, she checked the various agents on staff, trying to find the right fit for the upcoming mission. She wanted experience but most of the field operatives at Gamma Alpha were relatively new.

She'd need to pick someone a touch on the green side. Providing they had a decent training record, she could work with it. For most of them, it would only be their second or third time out. *At least they won't be going alone*, Christina thought. *That'll help. Well, fortune favors the bold . . . and the expendable. Time to give someone the bad news about how cold they'll be.*

***

Cassie contacted Salina from engineering, sending her the figures from their shield tests. She needed someone to double check their work, to confirm their findings. It wouldn't take long. Hopefully, they'd have the full results before arriving on Earth. Webber wanted to present them to Doctor Harper.

"Hi, Cassie," Salina said. "How's it going down there?"

"We've wrapped up our tests," Cassie replied. "I've sent you the results. Can you please double check them?"

"No problem." Salina paused. "Yep, they're here. So hey . . . are you standing in private?"

"Yes," Cassie paced out of earshot from the nearby technicians. "Webber's in his office. What's up?"

"We've been so busy, I haven't had a chance to ask you." Salina lowered her voice to a whisper. "How're things between you and Commander Bowman?"

Cassie's cheeks burned. "I'm . . . probably not at liberty to discuss that."

"So we should have lunch while we're waiting for the next op? If I want to hear about it that is."

"You never struck me as being interested," Cassie replied. Indeed, Salina didn't really get overly emotional on the bridge. Even when they were working together, she always remained neutral. The fact she wanted to know about a potential romance going on seemed especially shocking.

"Well, I am. And I'd love to hear more. I'll buy?" Cassie chuckled. "Okay, okay. When we're in orbit and things are settled, I'll happily do the lunch thing with you."

"Perfect!" Salina cleared her throat. "I've got one more personal question then I'll leave you alone, I promise."

Cassie smirked. "Go ahead."

"How're you feeling? You went down for that op . . . fought that guy . . . you've been inside the Orb. It makes me tired thinking about your adventures."

"I'm good," Cassie replied. "Though I have a bad feeling that when we arrive back on Earth, I'm going to be waylaid by Doctor Harper. I understand she tried to keep me from going on the last mission. She thought that after my contact with the Orb, I should've stayed on Earth under observation."

"What about Geoff?"

Salina was talking about Gunnery Sergeant Geoff Heathrow. He'd also been involved with the Orb but he went on the operation and descended to the planet as well. He and his unit fought there, taking out both Kalrawv soldiers and Tol'An. It was an intense bunch of fighting and didn't seem to be any worse the wear.

Aside from injuries sustained in battle at least.

"I don't know," Cassie said. "I'm sure she pushed for him to stick around too. Gil did but that was so he could work on the interface device. She's just trying to look out for us. There weren't research opportunities in us staying. But honestly, I felt fine and *needed* to be on that operation. It was important."

"I was glad to have you along. Thanks for the chat, Cassie. I'll check your figures right away."

"Thanks." Cassie cut the connection, heading over to Webber's office. "I'm heading up to my quarters. Salina's got the figures and will check them now."

"Appreciate it," Webber called over his shoulder. "I probably won't see you until we're on planet so have a safe trip when you head down."

"You too."

Cassie made her way through the ship and into her room, flopping on the bed. While she claimed to feel fine, there were side effects she didn't want to talk about. Sleep came differently for her than it had prior to interfacing with the Orb. It was like some of the connection, the information itself, lingered, impacting her rest.

She woke refreshed, but far more than ever before in her life, she experienced fantastically vivid dreams. Some were frightening, other inspirational but each felt as if she lived in those made up worlds. They reminded her of the vision she had when they first traveled back to Earth with an Orb in their possession.

How different is my mind now that I've been around these things for so long? The question had been bothering her for a while. Had she been altered by the Orb or simply fixating on the alien nature of the connection? She couldn't say for sure and the doctors claimed there was no *physical* ramification from her time with the devices.

That led her to ask a harder question. Had the Orbs altered her consciousness? Modified some intangible part of her? Even thinking it made Cassie feel like she was indulging a fantasy, a concept far removed from any provable science. *For now*. That thought gave her chills.

They already knew the Orbs held on to advancements they could only dream of. The interface method alone suggested heightened psychic abilities. If one were to believe in that, then one would have to believe in possibilities. And were they endless? As far as humanity was concerned just then, yes.

Whether or not that meant Cassie would understand exactly what happened to her within her lifetime was another story entirely. The key focus for their research involved gathering as much data from the Orbs as possible for defense and offense against their opponents.

Secondarily, they needed to worry about what caused the extinction of the race of beings who created the Orbs in the first place.

If they're even dead. One theory dancing about was that they may have elevated themselves to some other form of life, much like a previous mission where another race did so. They copied themselves into computers but what marvels could be? What could they have done to themselves?

There was some evidence of a plague, something that drove technology mad. A horrifying computer virus, one that humanity and the Pahxin both had to worry about returning. Without a sample of the data, they couldn't protect themselves, not entirely, but it seemed likely it was gone, never to return.

Of course, that might be wishful thinking. The horrors Cassie witnessed in her first vision haunted her to that day. She woke with a start in her bed, nearly falling to the floor. Someone was buzzing her door and that's what snatched her from sleep, pulling her out of what promised to become a second look at the darkness that befell that culture.

Cassie stood, frowning at the sweat making her shirt cling to her back and chest. Her hair was soaked but the buzz happened again. She would've rather avoided being seen bedraggled but it probably didn't matter. No one reported to her so she didn't necessarily have to put on a solid front at all times.

She opened the door. Vincent was standing there. His smile faded when he saw her. "Hey," he touched her arm, "are you okay?"

Cassie nodded. "Yeah, I'm good. I was just sleeping."

"More bad dreams?"

"It took a turn for the worst," Cassie replied, "but you woke me up before it could really get going."

"I've got good timing them." Vincent stepped inside. He tried to pull her close but she resisted.

"I'm disgusting, Vincent." Cassie stood back and looked down at herself. "Seriously, I don't even get how this happened. Anyway, I need to get cleaned up before we get there . . . Unless we're already home?"

"We'll take orbit in a half hour," Vincent replied. "So we've got time. I thought you might be hungry."

Even him saying that made her stomach growl. "I guess I am. I'll meet you in the cafeteria in a few minutes, huh? I just want to wash up and change."

"Sounds good." Vincent paused at the door. "You don't want some help with that whole cleaning thing, do you?"

Cassie laughed but waved her hand at him. "Get out of here, you maniac. We don't have time if we want to eat before having to head down. I'll talk to you in a few minutes."

He left and she went about preparing for the rest of her day. After a quick shower, she brushed through her short hair, staring into the mirror. Vincent proved to be the best thing that happened to her since she joined the Gnosis. Career advancement aside, she felt like the two of them genuinely came away with something special.

Cassie smiled at the thought. It felt nice to think of something besides galactic affairs, ancient civilizations and the impact super technology had on the common person. Considering the romantic part of her life, putting some of that into perspective, gave her hope. If they were fighting for anything, it was the right to be people, regardless of the world around them.

That's why she boarded the Gnosis and why she willingly took personal risks on their missions.

Chapter 2

Cassie approached Doctor Harper's lab, preparing herself for a potential tongue lashing. The scientist vehemently fought against Cassie's participation in the last mission and lost. How much that would impact her attitude remained to be seen. She tended to be all business but when emotions got involved, logic went out the window.

"Wait up!" Desmond's voice caught her off guard. Cassie glanced back at him as he ran to catch up. "You get summoned to the lair of the mad scientist too, huh?"

Cassie shrugged. "I guess so. Probably to see what Gil came up with while we were gone. Thayne's in there too. Maybe we can access the inner workings of the Orbs without having to risk a mental meltdown, huh?"

"That would be nice," Desmond said. They started walking together. "This shouldn't take too long. I've got a briefing with Reach about what we just did and what we're about to do. Gnosis repairs are almost complete. We need to refuel and we're out of here. I'd say we're pretty close to settling this affair for good."

"We're just going alone this time, right?" Cassie asked. "The Stalwart isn't joining us?"

"It's an abandoned station in the middle of nowhere," Desmond said. "And before you give me that look, I know. If it was that easy, how's the Orb not been found already, right? Intelligence suggests that no one's been out there for a long time. Pahxin cataloged it as some failed experiment from an ancient civilization."

"And no one's been out there?"

Desmond shrugged. "They can't really know that one way or another, I'm sure. But during the briefing, we'll hear from their intel people. We can put some questions to them then. You're welcome to come if you'd like."

Cassie lifted her brows. "I thought that was military and officers only?"

"Dulain will be there. I figure if your boss can sit in, so can you. Senior agent and all that."

"I'd like to hear the plan, sure. Especially if there's more information about the area. I might be of some help." Cassie paused before the door, putting her hand on his arm. "When we get this Orb, when we bring them all together . . . do you really think we're going to find the Tol'An? And if we do, what's the plan? Attack? Or let the Pahxin do it?"

"I don't know about you," Desmond replied, "but I fully intend to see this through."

Cassie nodded. "It would be a shame to let them wrap it up after all we've done but . . . on the flip side . . . we don't exactly have a military vessel."

"You guys are working on the shields. The weapons. When the time comes, we'll be able to participate. Trust me." Desmond gestured for the door. "Shall we? Doctor Harper might not complain about your participation in the mission now, but if we're tardy, it might give her enough fire to bring it all up."

"Fair point." Cassie tapped the panel to open the door and strode in. Technicians bustled about, shouting at each other over the beeps from computers and grinding power tools. Gil, Thayne, and Harper stood at a table in the center of the room, deep in a conversation. "Then again, she probably wouldn't have even noticed."

Gil held a metal box and he gestured at it firmly several times while speaking. The other two nodded as if their heads were on springs, each wearing a stern expression. Cassie turned to Desmond and shrugged. They advanced together to interrupt the confab to get their own meeting started.

"Hey there," Desmond said. His voice made Gil stop in the middle of a sentence. "Sorry, we were supposed to meet you here for a briefing?"

Harper snapped her fingers. "I nearly forgot! Thank you for coming. Please, join us. Gil was just explaining the structure of the device we're building to interface with the Orbs. It's a marvel. Absolute genius and we didn't even have to find a new material to make it work. We're making great things happen here, Captain. Absolutely great."

"Glad to hear it," Desmond replied. "I believe Webber sent down some figures about our shields and some other things. Have you been able to look at those? Is the new Orb nestled up next to its buddies? How're we doing?"

"We received the figures," Thayne said, "and I ran some preliminary tests. They look good. I think we can make the modifications he's talking about. I've got the computer testing it right now just to be sure we don't cause any serious problems . . . like the destruction of the module or all the generators."

"That would be bad," Cassie agreed. "What's the deal with this device? How long before it's done?"

Gil spoke up, "I'm still working on the case for it. While it may not initially be big enough, I wanted to know that we could create something capable of containing the energy required and still able to be handled by one of us. You see, it may produce a tremendous amount of radiation and, as you know, that would be bad."

"Indeed," Desmond replied. "Okay, so we're getting closer on that. The Orbs are all good. Shields might be upgraded before we leave. All this sounds great. Was there something else we need to talk about?"

Thayne said, "you are going to that outpost in the middle of nowhere, right?"

Desmond nodded. "That's the plan."

"I believe Gil was hoping to go on that mission and see it for himself."

"Isn't he working on this device?" Cassie asked.

"I am," Gil replied, "but Thayne can take over for me. This is a chance to see something truly unique, a structure left behind by a culture no one really knows about. At least, we didn't know about it until recently."

Desmond quirked a brow. "What does that mean?"

"I assume you haven't been to a briefing yet," Gil replied, "but apparently, the Pahxin government found out about the place a week or so back. They sent technicians to bring it online. They thought it would make a good research facility. Perhaps even a beacon to help locate criminals and enemies."

"Great." Desmond sighed. "We thought we were going to an abandoned facility."

"What's wrong?" Cassie asked. "If the Pahxin government knew about it, doesn't that mean they probably already have the Orb?"

Desmond shook his head. "Maybe but doubtful or they would've said so. More importantly though, if they found it, that means other people probably have too. That includes folks like the Tol'An . . . Kalrawv . . . pirates. God knows who else. We could be going into a real shit show if you'll excuse the vulgarity."

"The shields will be important then," Thayne added.

"And I will go with you?" Gil asked. "I want to see the base first hand."

"Yeah, you can come along if no one objects."

Harper grunted. "I seem to recall *my* objections didn't mean much when I pushed to have Agent Alexander remain behind last time."

"Sorry about that," Cassie muttered.

"Anyway," Desmond said. "We weren't trying to shut you out, Doctor Harper. But Cassie was needed on that mission. She's an expert and believe me, we needed everyone on board who could help." He turned to Gil. "Get your gear and be ready to depart in forty-eight hours. Cassie and I are going to a briefing now to find out about this . . . tech crew I guess."

"Is there anything else you want to show us?" Cassie asked.

"Not now," Harper replied, "but I'd appreciate it if you could stick around for a few minutes. We've got some leftover time from this meeting." She turned to Desmond. "If that's okay with you?"

Desmond smiled. "That's on Cassie. See you guys later." He took off. Harper motioned for Cassie to follow her.

"How'd the assignment go for you? How'd you feel?"

"Fine," Cassie replied. "Things are great."

"Yes? No ill-effects? Nothing strange?"

Cassie considered her answer carefully. If she was honest, would it prevent her from going on the next mission? Could anything stop her from boarding the Gnosis? A severe issue might. Did her dreams qualify? They didn't impact her performance nor did they bother her while she was awake.

"My dreams have been vivid," Cassie said. "Far more than ever before. Did . . . did Gil mention that?"

Harper nodded. "Yes. We've talked about it extensively as well. We believe the Orb has opened your consciousness, unlocked some part of your mind. That's why the dreams are more intense. Your mind is able to formulate the images, the fantasies. Gil believes that it would even be possible to unlock some form of precognition."

"Seriously?" Cassie frowned. "I don't know. I mean, we saw the past, sure . . . but the future? That seems farfetched even for super science. After all, the visions we had made sense. Those are recorded, maybe even by the Orbs. But beyond an intuition? Developing instinct? I can't see precognition."

"You may be right," Harper replied. "It's definitely still in the debate phase but that's what we do. Discuss a vision, test the vision, prove or disprove the possibility and move on to the next. It's an exciting time. However, back to your dreams. Gil is convinced that they are not dangerous but if anything else happens, please let us know right away."

"Of course."

"You should start writing down your dreams. If they're not too personal, I'd like you to share them. That would help us pinpoint if there are any similarities between you, Heathrow and Gil. If there are, then there might be more going on than simple dreaming. You do feel refreshed when you wake up, right?"

"Yeah, it's like the best sleep I've ever had."

"Fringe benefit, I suppose." Harper smiled. "Thank you, Agent. We'll look forward to your next report and good luck on the mission. From what I understand, we're getting close to being done with all this nonsense so we can get back to study, exploration and science."

"That's what I hear." Cassie nodded. "Good afternoon." She left, pausing in the hallway. The events in her dreams hadn't seemed particularly noteworthy. They were intense, yes, but not wild. Some of them were a touch personal . . . in ways she didn't want to talk to Harper about but most, she could discuss.

I wonder if they're going to bother Heat with this request. Cassie figured he would groan about having to write down his dreams. All things considered, it would be the simplest assignment he'd been given in a long time . . . and likely the hardest for him to get done. The marine didn't seem the type to do a lot of writing.

Nor sharing of his feelings for that matter. Cassie concurred. She didn't look forward to her next talk with the doctor, nor did she like the talk of further experimentation. They wouldn't be doing it with her, but whoever they suckered into it might very well find themselves in a lot of danger.

The mind was a complex, fragile thing. Pushing the limits with alien tech felt irresponsible. Hopefully, someone would find a way to regulate their probes but just then, the order of the day was winning a conflict against the terrorists. Everything else took second place to that, even safety.

***

Vincent arrived at the briefing, surprised to find several Pahxin representatives sitting around the table. Admiral Reach was already there but Desmond had yet to arrive. He took a seat, plugging his tablet into the table to tap into the meeting notes. The mission was supposed to be a cakewalk but something must've come up.

Otherwise, they would've only been meeting with the admiral.

When Dulain came in, Vincent knew the Gnosis was in for a lot more than they bargained for. *So much for the easy cruise.*

"Commander Bowman," Dulain said. "Good to see you."

"How're things going, Mister Dulain? Did you make headway on the investigation?"

Dulain shrugged. "We're working on it. Top people and all that. You guys ready to make history? Give us the advantage we need to win this war once and for all?"

"I think we're pretty close," Vincent said. "Though I'm a little nervous about our audience." He looked at the others. "Can you guys talk about what you're doing here? Do you have news?"

"They do," Reach replied, "but they'll talk about it when everyone's here for the briefing. No sense in having them repeat themselves unnecessarily."

Vincent shrugged at Dulain but he figured the intelligence director knew more than he let on. He probably had all the information about the Pahxin's report and then some. What was he doing about the potential traitors? A local faction, terrorists or a militia, had to have been involved but they weren't the standard mercenaries.

None of the prisoners talked. That meant they were conditioned, zealous. Who could field such people? And how had they come to be in league with the Tol'An? Vincent hoped there wasn't a leak in Gamma Alpha but that seemed to be the only explanation. Unless of course the Pahxin had been infiltrated, bringing one of the Tol'An with them inadvertently.

Desmond stepped into the room and took a seat. Reach nodded at him. "I think we're all here. Let's begin. As you all know, the Gnosis would be traveling to an abandoned outpost, an alien station thought to be abandoned. Unfortunately, we have some bad news. The station was discovered by a Pahxin survey crew. They informed the government."

"So much for the big secret," Desmond said. "What did the government do?"

"They sent a tech crew," Reach replied. "That's why we've got a problem. Contact has been lost with that ship. They could've been hit by pirates, some tech problem or their communications may simply be down. Therefore, your assignment is now two-fold. We need to get the Orb, but we also have to find the crew and rescue them if possible."

"Sounds easy enough," Vincent said. "How many could there possibly be?"

"Twenty-five," Reach said. "They were there to bring the entire station back online. Their ship carried several valuable parts as well. It's important that we get that back."

"Are we concerned about opposition?" Desmond asked.

"We should assume there will be, yes." Reach turned to his monitor. "Unfortunately, we have no more specific data about that situation. You'll be our eyes and ears. To that end, we're going to add some marines to the roster. Doctor Harper's team has finished up some additional power armor suits to take along."

"And we're restocking our fighters?" Desmond asked. "We lost a few in the last operation."

"Yes, we're good to go there." Reach looked at the Pahxin. "Do you have anything you'd like to add?"

"No, sir." One in the middle spoke. "You've covered all we know. Please get our technicians back. They're family people. A couple of them were in the military but they are not fighters anymore. Most are simple workers and we're fearing the worst for their lives. If you were to aid in their safe return, we would be most grateful."

"We'll do what we can," Desmond replied. "I'm getting the impression you guys are intent on this being something more than just a malfunction or environmental hazard. The chances are good we're looking at a technical failure that claimed their lives. If the original intelligence is to be given any weight that is."

"In which case," Reach said, "you'll be reporting the loss and collecting our cargo. But if not . . . and there is a force holding those people, then by God, you'll do whatever it takes to get them back."

Vincent understood the gravity of that statement and just what it meant. He hadn't heard such strong words since he joined the Gnosis. Then again, they hadn't set out to deal with hostages before. He figured the approach came from what happened when the Tol'An kidnapped Reach and the Pahxin ambassador.

I guess he knows what it's like so is willing to do whatever it takes. Vincent appreciated the fact they took the gloves off but it didn't bode well that they had to.

***

Desmond walked out of the briefing with Vincent and they headed for the cafeteria. Cassie caught up to them as they walked, calling out for them to hold up. "Hey! Did I miss the briefing?"

"Afraid so," Desmond said. "Turns out we're going into a potential hostage situation. It'll be a rough time but we're getting extra people for it."

"Great." Cassie frowned. "I have a meeting with Dulain later . . . but I don't think it has anything to do with that. Do you want me to ask him anything?"

Desmond shrugged. "Probably won't matter too much to be honest. We've got everything we need right now. Intel is crap, unfortunately, and we're about to walk into a situation where we may or may not have enemy combatants. From thinking we're heading out to a deserted facility to a fight."

"That's the story of our lives at this point," Vincent muttered.

They all started walking together. "I've got an update about crew numbers," Desmond said. "We're good on the marines. Heat's recovered sufficiently enough to feel ready for the next mission but that's between him and Fielding at this point. Pilots are good as well. Now if we only knew who we were fighting, I think we'd be in great shape."

"Do you think we don't know who we're facing then?" Cassie asked. "Surely, it has to be the Tol'An."

"They'd have the Orb and be gone by now," Vincent said. "It's got to be something else."

"We've run into enough strangeness out there to know this could be anything." Desmond smiled. "But let's be optimistic. With any luck, we'll find those guys have a broken transmitter and can't get it fixed. Sad for the Pahxin technicians but great news for us. Otherwise . . ."

"We'll be in a fight for our lives," Vincent finished.

"Think about this," Cassie said. "If this is the last mission before the final fight, if this leads to the conclusion of the Tol'An, then of course it won't be easy. I've been thinking about fate and destiny recently." Desmond raised a brow and she quickly nodded. "I know how that sounds, I blame Doctor Harper. But hear me out.

"Things might happen because they're supposed to. That deserted place suddenly becomes a hotbed of activity? Pretty convenient coincidence. I hate to be metaphysical, but maybe the universe thinks we need one more trial before this thing can end. Maybe one last struggle is what we need to be ready for the final fight and the Orb is the prize."

Vincent turned to Desmond. "What do you think?"

"I think you can call it whatever you want," Desmond replied. "Even if you don't believe in a higher power, the Orbs certainly have taught us enough about super science to believe in *something*. Whether or not the universe is testing the human race, I don't know but I'm pretty sure we'll overcome whatever it throws at us. One way or another."

"I'll eat lunch to that," Vincent said. "You guys game?"

"Yeah." Desmond nodded. "Let's drop the heavy talk for a while. We'll have plenty of time for that later."

Chapter 3

Ezria stood in his chambers, staring out the window at the crashing waves of the ocean some three hundred yards away. The tranquil scene gave him a sense of gravity, making him feel small amidst such natural fury. As the tides shifted, he accepted the reminder that he was indeed a tiny thing in an unfathomably massive universe.

News came in from the operation against the Kalrawv Group. His people failed to recover the Trindisha. He had not received word about Gizan. If the assassin had not died, he would wish he had. The punishment for a second failure would not be nearly as generous as the first. Even so, the thought was painful.

Ezria knew Gizan since before rising to power. He'd become friends with the man . . . or at least, as much as a leader could, given the circumstances of their organization. They had done great things together, pushed the influence of the Tol'An far beyond what any could've imagined. And now, as the humans entered the scene, Ezria's champion began to fail.

What did this mean? He communed with the Trindisha on the subject, to understand how this fledgling race barely reaching the stars could possibly stand against their might. He did not find any answers, none suitable. The mere fact they succeeded at all confounded him. Had they not allied with the Pahxin, he was fairly convinced they would've fallen.

Their friends are their strength. That gave Ezria comfort. It meant they were not as dangerous as he gave them credit for. One more Trindisha remained loose in the universe, a final opportunity for the Tol'An to consolidate their hold on the devices. With two in their possession, they were already incredibly dangerous.

Four would've made them unstoppable.

The two we have makes us a force to be reckoned with. I will have to sacrifice one to prove the point, however. Destroy the Pahxin homeworld perhaps . . . or maybe Earth. Those would both present them with a definitive example of what we're willing to accomplish and how far we're willing to go to bring order to them all.

But Ezria found it difficult to destroy one of the objects. He didn't hold any particular passion for them, no love for the information stored within. At least, he thought that might be true. Recently, after spending so much time meditating on them, he developed a possessiveness about them, a desire to keep them close.

The thought of sacrificing even one of them caused his heart to ache. *Will I be able to part with it when the time comes?*

"Master." A voice interrupted his thoughts and he turned to look at the soldier standing at attention. "I bring news from the last operation."

"Report."

"Lord Gizan has been declared dead. We lost nearly eighty-percent of our forces on the operation."

"Any captured?"

"Negative. According to our spies, several took their own lives."

"Including Gizan?" Ezria lifted his brows. "Do the enemies have his body?"

"Um . . . no, sir. It must have been obliterated during the fighting. It was not recovered by either side."

Ezria stepped away, staring out the window again. Gizan was crafty, a dangerous man. If there was any chance the man could've survived, he might have. The question was whether or not he would return to the Tol'An after failing. He'd been the most loyal of followers but after spending time in a cell, could his devotion have faltered?

"Send in General Trall," Ezria said. "Right away."

"Yes, master." The man clapped his fist to his chest before backing out of the room.

Ezria needed to ensure the trip to the space station proved fruitful, that they succeeded at something. There was also the matter of finding Gizan. Whether he chose to betray the cause, had been captured in a way that escaped the spies or was actually dead, his fate needed to be confirmed.
If Gizan chose to betray the Tol'An, he would be a painful thorn to contend with. Ezria wondered if they had anyone available who would be capable of tracking him down, of stopping him should he prove to be a problem. Hopefully, the general would have some suggestions.

Somehow, they needed to know the assassin was out of the picture.

General Trall entered the room, bowing his head briefly before approaching. He shaved his black hair so only stubble remained on his scalp. Tall, muscular and tough, he wore the scars of his office proudly on his face and hands. As a former officer of the Pahxin military, he was an excellent commander.

Had he not been disgraced for the murder of innocents, he might still be working for them. The Tol'An rescued him gave him a purpose and let him know they approved of a man's ability to make difficult decisions. Trall stood by his actions for his new people and his trained military proved successful until recently.

Time to give him a chance where Gizan failed. It was true, Trall had yet to meet the humans in combat. He worked over plenty of Pahxin patrols. He knew their tactics, used their predictability against them but in a subtle enough way to avoid them changing things up. If they knew who they were facing, they were fools.

"I have an assignment," Ezria said. "Undoubtedly you have heard about Gizan."

"Only that he has yet to return," Trall replied. "It is assumed he died."

"I'm not as easily swayed toward that. In fact, I think he may have betrayed us."

Trall shook his head. "Surely not. He is a loyal subject of the Tol'An. Our blade in the darkness."

"Who fell to disgrace with his first failure," Ezria pointed out. "Compounded by a second that cost us another Trindisha." He shook his head. "No, I feel we must find the right people to track him down. Find him, or his body. Return them here. If he is dead, we can put him with the fallen. If not . . ."

"We will execute him for his failure," Trall spoke firmly, practically spitting the words out. Apparently, his distaste for treason rivaled Ezria's. "Pardon me for asking, but do you believe that he would attempt to stop us from our own work? That he would stand in the way of our success?"

"Depending on how he feels," Ezria said, "he may do a number of things. I do not trust him now. His failure may have been purposeful but our spies are not able to confirm that. I doubt the humans were able to simply overpower his people, kill them all and take the Trindisha. That seems highly unlikely."

"To me as well." Trall scowled. "Our people were mismanaged during that operation, that much I do know."

"Do you believe you will do better?"

Trall seemed to weigh his response, taking several moments before answering. "I know I will. Once I have the opportunity to field a force against the aliens, these . . . rat humans . . . I will annihilate them."

"Then you will have your wish soon," Ezria replied. "I have sent a destroyer to a distant space station far from here . . . another Trindisha. When they return, we will be ready to launch a full-scale attack on our enemies. Can I trust you to be a light in the darkness? The man to bring honor to our cause?"

"You can, Master Ezria!" Trall slapped his fist against his chest.

"Then go." Ezria pointed. "And don't forget, I want someone assigned to find Gizan. His body must be located . . . or his head should it be attached to a live being."

"Of course, My Lord." Trall departed and Ezria returned to watching the water hit the rocks. Yes, the universe might be massive, it may even make a single individual feel insignificant but when the Tol'An won the war, things would be different. History would know the true leader of all sentient beings and then, he would not feel so small.

* * *

Squadron Leader Dennis Arden headed to the hangar, adjusting his flight suit along the way. Someone nudged him in the hallway. Lieutenant Alicia Quinn grinned at him. "Sorry, sir. You looked a little serious for your own good."

"I didn't like the briefing," Dennis said. "Too many unknowns. Might not matter to us but I can't imagine the soldiers are going to have a good time of it."

"Ah." Alicia nodded. "I see. I thought it might've been something else."

Dennis lifted his brows. "What then?"

"Dala." Alicia looked away. "I figured you were thinking about her."

Dennis felt his cheeks warm. He drew a deep breath. "Yeah, a little. I guess I've been wondering what she's up to. What assignment did the Stalwart take? Is she being just as wildly reckless?"

"That worry you?" Alicia asked.

"Yeah, it does." Dennis smirked. "Kind of ridiculous, huh? She's more than capable. Hell, she made it this far without backup from me. I've been struggling to come to terms with their method of warfare but I bet you get it. You're practically an honorary member of their pilot battalion."

"I like to get things done, true." Alicia winked. "But hey, you're trying to change the subject. Are you going to pursue the girl?"

"That doesn't seem practical." Dennis shook his head. "No, I think it would be best if I kept things platonic. How would we keep in touch even? At some point, they'll assign a different ship to work with us and we'll be separated anyway. No, I'm pretty sure that we had our brief moment . . . and it's probably over."

"I dunno. People find a way if they want to," Alicia replied. They arrived at the hangar doors. "I wouldn't give up if I was you. No reason. Give it a try. Have hope. It's one of the reasons we're out here looking for that damn Orb. Why the marines go into those ridiculously dangerous locations."

"I appreciate your perspective." Dennis patted her on the shoulder. "Sincerely. Now, I think we've got somewhere to be. See you out there. Maybe you won't have to show off any of those heroics you're so keen on, huh?"

"There's always room for those," Alicia said. "You just have to know how to look for them. Good luck, sir. Talk to you soon."

***

Desmond sat in his office on the Gnosis, going through the reports. Everyone showed ready, supplies were full and it was just a matter of timing before they left on the mission. He had made a request to get the Stalwart as support for the mission but it was denied. Even with the potential Tol'An and other unknown threats, high command had faith the Gnosis would be sufficient.

He hadn't told Vincent or anyone else of their decision. He figured it didn't matter. Tweaks to the shields and weapon systems made them far more deadly than their last encounter with the Kalrawv Group. And those people used experimental equipment, state of the art offensive and defensive gear that probably hadn't even been properly tested.

Scavengers, pirates or other fringe groups might stand a chance against the Gnosis but Desmond wasn't worried about facing them. His primary concern rested on the unknown, the things they couldn't quantify. Why was the station abandoned? Who left it behind? They had enough stories about ancient civilizations to be leery of that element above all else.

"Captain," Zach's voice crackled over the speaker. "This is the bridge, do you copy?"

Desmond tapped his tablet to acknowledge. "I'm here. What's up?"

"We are in position for hyperspace. Coordinates are fed into navigation, control has cleared us and we're ready to go on your mark."

"Initiate the countdown," Desmond said, "I'll be up there in just a moment." He killed the connection and headed for the bridge. Zach and Salina suggested they would only be in hyperspace for five hours, which proved to be a dramatic improvement over how long such trips took before.

Through the optimization that was meant to put them in the hands of the Tol'An, and modifications through Pahxin assistance, they had dramatically improved their hyperdrive performance. A couple more generations of hyperdrive module and faster than light travel would become a viable military tactic.

At least when combat happened in systems with close enough proximity. A twenty-minute hop between one solar system and the next could turn the tide of a battle, especially if an entire fleet could make the journey. Though the Pahxin had yet to perfect such technology, multiple Orbs might just make it happen.

Desmond stepped onto the bridge when they had just reached the one-minute mark. He took his seat beside Vincent who leaned close, speaking quietly. "Pilots are prepped. When we're a half hour away from emerging, they'll mount up and be ready for launch upon arrival. Two wings should be able to patrol the area after our initial scans."

"Perfect. I've asked Captain Gabriel to ensure the marines get plenty of rest. They might have a rough time of it when they board the shuttle." Desmond considered his comment for a moment. "We need to get as much data about that thing before anyone goes over there. Get with Salina and Cassie to ensure they have a solid plan."

"You think we have to worry about interference again."

"It's another unknown place. God knows what we have to deal with. I just want to be prepared." Desmond smirked. "Gil will probably want in too. Make sure he knows."

"He's requested to go with the marines."

"Hm." Desmond wanted to ensure the place was safe before he sent any unarmored personnel over but he understood Gil's desire. The man knew more about ancient cultures than anyone they had access to. Even if that didn't matter for the assignment per se, it would help them understand the station better and potentially locate the Orb quicker. "Second unit."

"After the place is secure?"

"At least a beachhead." Desmond turned to the main screen as Zach reached the thirty second mark. "Alright, folks. Here we go."

This may well be our last military operation before the final battle. Desmond thought. *I can't believe we're so close. We've got this, people. We've got this.*

***

Salina glanced at the viewscreen as it came online but only just long enough to see something real. Emerging from hyperspace didn't particularly bother her, not to an extent of feeling fear or struggling with nerves. However, deep in the hindbrain, she needed to witness some reality before diving into the scans and computer data.

Once she got that brief ritual out of the way, she dove into her duties of checking their immediate area for threats and to double check Zach's assessment on the success of their navigation. The first thing to pop up on her screen was the station, some two hours away from their current location.

Other than that, nothing seemed to be moving in the system, no other ships, no vessels . . . not even debris. That struck her as odd, especially considering what they'd seen in every other place they'd visited. Compared to the last hectic location, this one was positively tranquil.

Way too suspicious. Salina directed the scans to the station. Power emanated from within, easily enough to power the whole thing. *Maybe those technicians got the place back online. Unless the people who left it did so in such a hurry that they left the lights on. Possible, but unlikely.*

There were multiple ships docked with the station as well, different varieties. One she found in the database right away. It was the Pahxin government ship, built for repairs and recovery. The people they were looking for remained. Whether they were alive or not, that was another story.

Despite the fact that the scanner picked up the power source, it did *not* find any life forms. *How can I find one but not the other? Is the reactor really* that *powerful? Hm.* Salina turned to Cassie. "Are you checking for the Orb? I've got their reactor but something's blocking life signs."

"No, I don't." Cassie frowned. "There are only two planets orbiting the star in this system and the station isn't anywhere near them. It seems they're dead. The Orb *must* be on the station if it's out here at all. It's more than possible someone else found it already. The thing should be pumping out *something*."

Salina added, "the station's maintaining position artificially. I wonder how long it's been here like this."

"We'll close in," Desmond said. "Will you be able to determine if the station's safe to board? Power armor will protect the marines but a virus might explain the lack of life readings."

"Yes, and no," Salina replied. "Our instruments are sensitive enough that they should be picking up something as subtle as a virus again. But I'm not detecting interference of any kind."

"What about those three ships?"

Salina sighed. "They're dead ends as well. All systems are functional but we're receiving no data."

Vincent said, "that may be why these ships docked. They thought there was nothing to worry about."

"Good point." Desmond tapped his com, establishing a connection with Captain Gabriel. "Darren, we're on the verge of deploying your people. Once the fighters finish their pass, we'll have the shuttles head in."

"Got it," Darren replied. "Anything to worry about?"

"Suspiciously, no." Desmond frowned. "Hopefully, the fighters will get us some more information. Either way, your guys will be our eyes and ears. I'll let you know shortly. Bradford out." He turned to Vincent. "Have we launched the fighters?"

Vincent nodded. "They're on their way. Should be at the station in less than five minutes at current speed."

"Zach, increase speed," Desmond said. "I want to be close enough for a rapid extraction if needed."

Salina fought back a surge of frustration. Every scan returned the same information, the same nothing. She tapped into the fighter com net, sending a message to their computers. When they passed by the station, their sensors would run a deep scan of the structure and send it directly back to her station.

She didn't hold out much hope but it was better than nothing.

Chapter 4

Squadron Leader Anna Jager was the first one out of the ship, taking her fighter out to the designated rendezvous. Her Charger unit would form up and take one side of the station while Mustang went on the other. Scans showed the area was blessedly clear of . . . well . . . anything but that felt flat out wrong.

Gnosis control confirmed what she saw. Anna turned her attention to the station, noting the closest ship docked to the thing. It was big, though not quite as large as the Gnosis. It definitely could've held at least a couple of fighters, though it would've been a tight fit. Her database didn't recognize the silhouette.

This gets better and better. Anna spoke to Flight Lieutenant Preston Everest, her second. "Got an opinion about all this?"

"It sucks?"

Anna smirked. "That was more direct than I expected." The rest of the unit formed up with them and they headed out on their patrol pattern. They would fly by two of the docked vessels. Maybe they'd see something on visual that the scanners were missing. Any activity aboard the ships would make the situation seem less eerie.

That's the problem, Anna thought. *This feels flat out creepy—more so than what we've seen so far.*

At first, the station looked like any other they'd seen so far. A technical marvel, hovering in deep space. But as they drew near, it became obvious there was something different about the surface. It was rigid, textured like some kind of reptile. When it caught the light from the distant star, it seemed to glisten.

They passed the first ship docked, the one with no silhouette. Lights emanated from different points across the hull, indicating it had at least minimal power. *So where are all the people?* Terrible thoughts filled her head as her imagination went wild. Disintegration, a horrible disease, and marauders all could've befallen the place.

But there was simply no indication of specifically what happened. They probably needed access to the station computer if they wanted to understand not only recent events but those in the past as well. What people built the structure and how was it maintained without manual intervention?

"You guys have anything on scans?" Anna asked, ensuring she was connected to Mustang as well. "I've got absolutely nothing."

"Same here," Dennis replied. "Ship on our side looks like it might be Tol'An though. No activity on board. Just a power source running hot."

"I'd say the marines should be good to go in then," Anna said. "Might be the only we'll get any answers about this place." She tapped into Gnosis control. "Command, we've scouted the area and it's clear. No activity on scans. Ships docked all seem to be fully functional and powered up but no souls on board we can detect."

"Keep flying your pattern," Vincent replied. "We're sending the marines in now to dock. You're the eyes out there. With scans being odd, it's important we maintain your presence. Let us know if anything changes."

"Will do." Anna returned the conversation to the others. "You heard him, folks. Sounds like we'll be out here a while longer. Stay alert. God knows when this might turn south on us. Especially if that's a Tol'An ship. I can't believe they just happened to be there then disappeared."

***

Heat sat on the shuttle, staring out the window as it took off. He thought about the situation, about injury and how insane their missions became. This one *seemed* straightforward but he didn't count on it. Something happened to all those people and they were about to find out what the hard way.

Gillet sat beside him along with a whole lot of newbies who hadn't been out of the solar system before. They seemed okay during the jump but flying the shuttle over, he could feel their nerves. Each of them may not have admitted to being scared but they'd have to turn on quite a bit of bravado to be convincing.

Heat came out with little more than bumps and bruises in the last mission. His old armor had to be retired. It saved his life, though he wasn't entirely sure how when he thought back on what happened to him. When he went to look at his armor, it shocked him he managed to walk to the armory.

Gillet nudged him. "You're not convinced this place is deserted."

"If it is, we're going to find a lot of bodies," Heat said. "Three ships worth. And what would've killed them? The Gnosis would've found radiation or contagions. No, I think something's found a way to mask scans and we're going to find a whole lot of people on the station causing havoc."

"So you're thinking we need to be prepared for a fight."

Heat nodded. "A big one."

"We're coming up on the station," the pilot's voice interrupted them. "Docking in less than five minutes. Get yourselves ready. Scans are still pulling nothing. Command is saying you'll want to tap into the first terminal you find and relay information. Speaking of which, Lieutenant Fielding is on the line."

"Hey guys," Fielding said. "Sorry I can't be out there with you. Doctors say I've got another few days before I can do combat ops again. That said, we all know this isn't as easy as it seems. When you get in there, I want you all to set up a perimeter around the airlock and start scouting the area. Push out into other modules slowly until we discover what happened."

"You don't want us to just go balls out?" One of the new guys, Private Hendricks said. "You know, dash out there and see what happens?"

"We don't need that, Private," Fielding said. "And keep the chatter down. I'm initiating a camera check right now." He paused. "Looks good. You're docking now. Act in unison, gentlemen. That goes for all you rookies. Follow your team leads and you'll be fine. This is just another assignment."

You know, Heat thought, *with a totally unknown force that we're about to face with zero intelligence on an alien facility. But yeah, totally normal. Just like a tour in the jungles of Africa. Relax about it.*

Heat exchanged a glance with Gillet. He had to be thinking the same thing.

The shuttle rattled as it settled against the station. The sides of the door slammed against the walls, creating a vacuum seal around the smaller entrance. Once they pressurized, they would pop the station door and gain access. When the hissing stopped, Gillet stepped forward and used his tablet, attempting entrance.

Heat watched him work and grew concerned when the man stood up straight. "What's up?"

"Looks like Pahxin codes," Gillet said. "That's odd. Maybe they *did* bring the station back online after all."

"They were a tech crew," Heat pointed out. "Does that mean you can open it?"

"Doing so now."

The door slid upward, revealing a hallway illuminated by dim lights overhead. Heat took a step out, checking his HUD for any changes in the air, anything to be concerned about. It read perfectly normal. The station module ahead looked large enough for at least Heat's team to stand inside.

"We're entering the station proper," Heat said over the com. "Probing other modules will begin soon. Has the other team docked? We need to sync up."

"They're docking now, Heat," Fielding said. "I'll get you guys hooked up. For now, secure the area. The shuttle will remain in place until you're done as a means for quick extraction so I want that area locked down. Leave guards."

"I'm on it." Heat turned to a couple of the new guys. "You stay here. No one gets to the shuttle. If it looks like you can't hold the line for any reason, inform the pilot and have him detach right away." He turned to Gillet. "Let's start scouting this place. Orb's gotta be here somewhere they figure."

"We'll find it." Gillet headed into the next module. "Though it might take a while. This place is huge."

"The other team will shorter work of it." Heat paused as his HUD glitched. He tapped his helmet and it steadied. "Odd. Did your tech just give you trouble?"

Gillet shook his head. "Nope, I'm good."

Heat nodded. He stepped into the module, taking in the smooth walls and grated floor. Darkness covered the floor beneath them but every footstep caused an echo, indicating at least several feet of open space beneath them. Three doors led off in different directions, deeper into the station.

The one on the left *seemed* like the best choice, though Heat had no idea why. It was literally a gut feeling, a moment of intuition. He thought about it for a brief moment and headed that way. His team fell in behind him and as he approached, the door slid open. The HUD picked something up, something organic.

Metal consoles stood in the center of the room, like computer banks surrounding a platform. A considerable amount of blood coated one of them, marring the floor. Heat stepped closer, crouching beside it. His HUD picked up a device nearby, some kind of small tablet. The screen was cracked but it still had a power source.

"Lieutenant," Heat said, picking it up. "I found something. I don't think I can access it here but maybe if we bring it back to the shuttle, the Gnosis can try something. Also, something did happen here. I found a lot of blood. No body."

"But scans aren't picking it up?" Fielding asked. "How'd you find the blood?"

"It was in the next room," Heat said. "But my scan only detected it when I got close enough to see. Looks like it's Pahxin for sure. I suppose it's possible they dumped the body out the airlock but I have a feeling we're going to find something horrifying in the place." He stood up. "We'll get the tablet back to the shuttle and continue our sweep."

***

Cassie continued pinging the area, hoping she missed something. Nothing came back, time and again. The marines entered the station and even so, their reports didn't show any additional information. She began to worry that the Orb had been moved, or even taken. The docked Tol'An ship indicated their enemies arrived ahead of them.

If they got the Orb, why would they abandon one of their ships? That didn't make any sense but the terrorists had shown their propensity for waste before. Perhaps the prize of gathering another of the devices outweighed the ship or maybe they lost enough people that they could only pilot one.

The questions annoyed her and there was no easy way to gather more data.

"Cassie," Salina said. "Heat and his team found a tablet on board. They've plugged it into the shuttle."

"Pahxin?" Cassie asked.

"Yeah. Cracked screen but the data seems to be okay. It's encoded." Salina grinned. "I thought you might want a chance to bust it."

"Thanks!" Cassie logged into the shuttle's computer then accessed the device. Whoever it belonged to used a simple password to protect their data. It didn't require any real hacking to get into it. Once a basic decryption program ran, she had access to an entire array of audio data.

Cassie put on her headset and brought up the first one, hitting play. She had to read subtitles for what he was saying in Pahxin. "My name is Zahl Dray, and I'm a pirate. Everyone needs to know what happened to my crew. This station is cursed. There is no other way to explain what I have seen."

The chilling message ended and Cassie turned to Desmond. "Captain," she said, "Heat and his crew found something big."

"Signs of the crew?"

"Maybe. An audio log from a pirate who boarded the station at some point. It was recorded somewhat recently." Cassie paused. "There's quite a bit here to go through but he did mention something about the place being cursed and that something happened to his crew. It sounds pretty bad."

"Okay, dive in." Desmond turned to Vincent. "Warn those marines. This sounds a little superstitious but better to be on the safe side."

Vincent spoke on the com for a moment. "They found blood over there."

"Lends some weight to the concern," Cassie said. "I'll listen ahead and see what I discover." She ran a program which would translate the recording and alter it to English on a separate track. That would be for a briefing later. Cueing up the next recording, she drew a deep breath and hit play.

***

The firing line drove back the attackers. Zahl noted his own people didn't make it out unscathed. He didn't even know who survived and who didn't. Chaos swept over the ranks and Captain Rand didn't seem to be doing anything about it. That's when he noticed his leader lying on his side, his stomach wide open.

He might've been unconscious but the injury would claim his life momentarily.

"What's going on?" The way the person screamed the question was so frantic, Zahl had no idea who asked. "What are those freaks? What're we doing?"

No one stepped up to give any orders but they all began to panic. A couple headed back toward the ship but they were barred. A brawl began. Some wanted to leave immediately, others demanded they claim the prize. They were there for the technical ship, not to flee empty handed.

Zahl recognized they didn't have the money to walk away but after the attack, he felt it would be wise to find easier prey elsewhere. However, throwing his voice into the midst of the others didn't make a lot of sense. They were arguing, not looking for solutions. And the fighting began a few moments after that.

A few shoves, some punches then the weapons came out. Half the crew burst off and went to a different module to confer. The others guarded the ship, trying to decide what to do. Zahl went with the cooler headed people, stepping away from their own vessel. He figured they needed a plan fast. The freaks who attacked them might be back at any moment. "I don't have to take your orders!" One man shouted. It led to a shoving match. Zahl backed away. They weren't behaving like themselves, not remotely. Rabble rousers had long since left the crew through various means. They mostly got along a few random disagreements aside.

Zahl hadn't seen such behavior since they first got together and no one trusted Rand. Had the captain's presence been so great that his death immediately made the crew fall apart? That didn't seem likely. And yet they were all behaving like idiots in the face of a real threat, a danger none of them understood.

They'd all seen irrational behavior on their jobs, but usually from their victims. The pirates had all been tested under fire. Not a man among them had gone away unscathed throughout their careers. Injuries could be survived and they recognized that. So what about this particular situation pushed them over the edge?

Perhaps the ferocity of their combatants, the people that charged them. Zahl never imagined he would witness such a spectacle of men throwing their lives away as they bolted for a firing line. The lack of self-preservation offered an intimidation value, one that was hard to ignore.

The bickering escalated as the crew divided up into two sides. One wanted to leave, the other demanded they stay. Violence became an option for both. Zahl stepped in, pointing out they had a common enemy somewhere else on the station. At first, they ignored him but then they agreed. Those killers should be hunted down.

"That's not what I'm saying!" Zahl shouted. "We should not risk our lives to fight with those maniacs. We can get out of here and find easier game. The captain would not want everything we worked so hard for to be dashed over a single job. We have a ship . . . We have the means to take another score. Let's go!"

"Vengeance!" They shouted the word in unison. Their eyes went wide and wild. They charged off into the station, leaving Zahl to stare after them in baffled shock. Not a single one hesitated except him. They were caught up in a severe bloodlust, a hunger for murder that none of them exhibited before.

"It isn't that bad!" Zahl shouted after them but they were already gone. If he could've flown the ship, he might've abandoned them. It wasn't an option. Resigned to watch the spectacle, he moved after them at a distance, to see what exactly would happen and whether or not they would succeed and murdering those who attacked them.

***

Cassie rubbed her eyes as the audio finished playing. Why would those men go to such an extreme? If the pirate's words were to be believed, then there was no reason for them to get so riled up. Perhaps something was released into the air during the violence, a chemical no one was looking for while the fighting raged.

She checked the scans of the station again, frowning at how little it came back with. Perhaps their sensors were simply not tuned to catch whatever occupied the station but she knew there was something. It was just a matter of figuring out how to measure it. She sent the transcript to Desmond then shared it with Salina as well.

The next audio file needed time to decompress. She occupied herself with probing different frequencies with her scanner, different methods of gathering data. Power armor protected against particulates but if the problem was not measurable, would it be hindered by technology?

Cassie needed to find out quickly to help those men and ensure they remained safe. With Salina's help, they might find something but they didn't have any time for trial and error. She needed to listen to more of the audio, to find out what happened next. Perhaps the answer would present itself there and give them a quick edge.

It might even lead to the discovery of the Orb. Cassie watched the percentage meter rise past eighty, tapping the console impatiently. Curse to her represented something the man didn't understand, a scientific explanation for strange behavior. The Orb taught her that some things might be beyond comprehension.

But probing led to answers. She simply needed to be willing to keep poking.

Chapter 5

Christina pulled Agent Sandoval Essex to accompany her on the mission. He'd been with the agency for just over a year. Before that, he'd been a marine with a solid record and over a dozen combat ops to his name. He'd never gone out alone but he expressed his confidence in what they were about to do.

She didn't particularly want to go with someone brand new. Part of her worried about their loyalty but she couldn't go down that path. If she didn't trust people within her own organization, then the AIA was in serious trouble. Even so, she double checked his records and ensured the details were accurate.

They didn't have time for a full vetting process. She met him in the hangar, geared up in a tactical suit complete with bulletproof padding on the chest and legs. A helmet provided access to her tablet as well as a HUD with scanning capabilities. She armed herself with a submachine gun, a pistol and two fragmentation grenades.

Sandoval stood around waiting for her. He dressed the same but he favored a larger assault rifle for his primary. He also carried more grenades, including some flashbangs. He stood at attention when she approached, his black hair barely grown out from having recently been shaved.

Brown eyes stared straight ahead, his dark skin seemed to be covered with sweat.

"You nervous about something, Agent?" Christina asked.

"No, ma'am!" Sandoval shouted.

"This isn't the marines." Christina passed him by and boarded the shuttle. "We can de-formalize a bit. Come on. We've got a long flight ahead of us."

Essex sat across from her, his posture textbook perfect. He looked like a marine recruitment poster. If he planned on sticking with the AIA, he needed to loosen up. Anyone would pick him out as a spy in about a minute and a half. Maybe he could stick to combat operations but that wasn't why most people joined them.

Christina tried to remember if she'd been so stiff when she first started. She remembered nerves, certainly but not specifically being so rigid and bound by military protocol. She'd always been a little defiant of authority. Pretending to be Major Dawson, working for the admiral, that had been the hardest ruse of her life.

"You should probably relax," Christina said. "This job's not about starched collars and getting to the mess hall on time."

"I'm trying to figure that out."

"What did you do in the marines? Combat unit?"

"Yes, ma'am."

Christina nodded. "Let's start with titles. Just call me *Christina*."

"Er . . . okay." Essex cleared his throat.

"So when you were out there putting boot to ass for your country, did you always follow protocol? I thought marines were all about improvising and overcoming obstacles. You know, facing down threats regardless of the circumstances."

"We definitely met any obstacle and defeated it, ma . . . Christina."

"Okay." Christina shrugged. "Just remember that everything you encounter in this position is totally out of the ordinary. It's coming from left field and will *not* let you follow a rule book or process. We're in the business of improv. Acting, what we do . . . hell, even this trip. Would you believe the plan to come out here was conceived about six hours ago?"

"So soon?"

"Yep. We need intel so here we are," Christina waved her hands about, "heading out to a god forsaken base in the middle of nowhere to check something."

"I'm not entirely sure I understand the mission," Essex said. "You mentioned we have a traitor? What're they doing? Who are they betraying us to?"

"They're somehow getting information to the terrorists, the Tol'An. I'm not sure how they even got a hold of them. There's a chance that we've been infiltrated by one of their agents . . . in which case, we have to root them out."

"Do you expect us to find them here?"

"Unfortunately, I can't be sure. We picked up a signal but scans aren't showing anything. They might be using advanced technology to hide." Christina smiled. "Visual is the only way to be sure. Even if they aren't there, we might find some evidence that will lead us to them."

"Wait . . ." Essex sat forward. "Beside the pilot, we're only going in there with two people? Where's our backup?"

"What's that?"

"Excuse me?"

Christina smiled. "We're the backup. Spies, remember? Go behind enemy lines, do crazy stuff, get the information we need . . . I picked you because you're highly trained and highly motivated. I hope I was right."

"You were, but . . ." Essex stared at the floor for a long moment. "I suppose I never imagined we would be going into a potential combat mission with only two people."

"Don't worry, if it's totally insane, we'll just extract and send in a team. Otherwise, this is all stealth. We shouldn't have too bad of a time."

The pilot called back to them. "We'll be at the drop off point in less than ten minutes. I'm going in low, below any scan range. Even advanced tech shouldn't grab us."

"Thanks," Christina said. She turned to Essex. "We'll have a bit of a hike but the shuttle will be nearby for a quick extraction if we need it."

"Great, I never mind a little winter stroll." Essex finally grinned. "I see why people don't complain about this job. It's more exciting than I thought it would be."

"Believe me, if I hadn't pulled you, I think you would've been doing evals and escorts for the better part of two years. Hopefully, we survive this thing and you get fast tracked for your efforts. Watch my back and you'll definitely have my recommendation. Hey, one more thing, don't hesitate to put a target down. We can get intel without them. Clear?"

"I have no qualms putting a target down."

Christina believed him. He might be green, he might've been too rigid but whenever they got marines, those men were capable of doing the dirtier parts of the job. It was the one thing trainers didn't have to push on them. Killing represented a habit they already possessed. AIA operatives tended to come from the tech or educational fields.

People like Cassandra Alexander were the type that tended to flourish in the AIA in peace time but wartime . . . Well, Essex had an advantage there.

The shuttle swooped low and remained hovering while the back doors dropped. Christina dropped the mask on her helmet, bringing up a HUD. The mountains stretched out to the left and right, pure snowy desolation all around them. She hopped onto the ledge, allowing her tablet to provide a path to their destination.

Essex stepped out behind her and the shuttle pulled away, remaining low and heading east. Christina pulled a com check before heading out. They had a two-mile hike to get to their destination. Providing their pilot proved to be correct about his approach, they should've had an advantage.

If he was wrong . . . they might just be walking into a real shit show.

***

Fielding listened to the briefing from Captain Gabriel concerning what happened to the pirates. He cursed under his breath, turning to address his men. Everyone knew there was some sort of unknown out there but this might've exceeded all concerns. Random, odd behavior brought on by something undetectable definitely did not make his list of potential issues.

"Heat, I've got some bad news." Fielding explained what they knew so far. "Agent Alexander's trying to find more data now but I don't know how long it's going to take. If you guys experience anything strange, I want you back at the shuttle immediately. Don't hesitate. Get me?"

"Understood." Heat sighed. "Was that a private message straight to me then?"

"It was."

"Got it." Heat turned to Gillet and tapped his helmet. "Go private, buddy."

"What's wrong?" Gillet asked. "Did they finally figure out what's going on here?"

"Partially. Enough to know that people went nuts for no conceivable reason yet." Heat gestured ahead of him. "Let's press on in that direction. I want to check the power core in this place. If the tech crew brought it back online, we'll know. Plus, that would be the most logical location for a device to block our scans."

"How so?"

"Stopping us from getting life signs?" Heat shook his head. "It would take a lot of energy to pull that off. Anyway, I'll lead the way." He took point, pressing through to the next module. The marines filed in behind him but he sensed a level of hyper-awareness in his men. They were definitely picking up the odd vibe and it manifested in nerves.

Heat's HUD picked up a vibration, some kind of noise roughly sixty yards to his left. The others started chattering about it so he knew he wasn't the only one. *I wonder if that would've counted for the type of strange behavior Fielding called out*. He altered course, moving to the left and pressing through the next door.

A beam of energy seared the wall not even six inches from his head. "Contact!" Heat shouted the word, dashing forward. The room he entered housed multiple computer consoles, each one no more than waist high. He dropped into a crouch to take cover. Gillet joined him while the others remained at the door, standing around the corner.

"Did you see them?" Gillet asked.

"No, and there's *still* nothing on scans." Heat lifted his weapon, aiming it over the console to use the camera on the weapon. He caught shadows moving against the wall. There were at least three people and they had enough sense to stay down. That didn't match up with what Cassie heard about in her audio file.

Maybe these are unaffected.

"Stand down!" Heat yelled. "We're not your enemies. Throw down your weapons and we'll talk about this!"

Weapons buzzed, casting beams that seared the metal walls around the door. Heat slipped to the side, remaining crouched. He saw the guns sticking out over the console and as he moved, he found an angle that afforded him a shot on one of their sides. He took aim and fired a burst.

The target screamed, blood splattered everywhere. Two men ran for the door. "They're running!" Heat shouted, firing after them. He caught one in the legs and before the other could make it out, Gillet popped him in the head. The two of them checked the bodies, finding them all quite dead.

"Clear!" Gillet called to the others. "For the moment. Lock this place down!"

Each body wore a blue jumpsuit with an insignia that Heat didn't recognize. He took a shot of it and sent it to Fielding. "Lieutenant, we've encountered a hostile force. They took some shots at us and we were forced to retaliate. Three down. No injuries on our side. I've sent you an image of one of their insignias. Can you please check the database?"

"I'm on it," Fielding said. "So you were in the room with them? Did they show up on your HUD?"

"No." Heat hesitated for a moment. "We're making our way to the power core of the station. I'm hoping we'll find a device that might be causing this . . . invisibility."

"Good idea. That insignia is Pahxin. Technical division of their government." Fielding sighed. "Did you just kill some of the men we were here to save?"

"Sir, they fired on us," Heat replied. "And they would not comply when asked to stand down. This was self-defense. They had zero interest in conversation."

"Understood, but this is still going to be a problem. We'll need some more evidence to prove they were in an odd state of mind. Do what you can, Heat."

"Gunny," Vine spoke up. "I've got some movement over here now. That same vibration . . . I guess footsteps on the deck?" He was indicating the direction they needed to go to get to the power core. Heat noticed it too, this time far more prominent than what drew them into the room with the tech guys.

Heat's HUD flickered and for a moment, he saw *dozens* of blips all around them on the scans. They were in every module less than a hundred yards away and they were closing in. Just as the scanner went blank again, people began to scream all around them. The cacophony rose until it became impossible to tell how many might be out there.

Why'd my HUD work for a moment? Heat shook his head. *We don't have time to worry about that.* "Fall back toward the shuttle!" He shouted. "Get your asses moving, people! Gillet and I have the rear now go!"

The marines fell out, rushing the way they'd come. Heat felt a rush of urgency as adrenaline filled his veins. His men moved quickly but being at the back of the line put him directly between them and a couple more random shots from their opponents. Once those people, if that's what they were, got a firing solution, he was pretty sure they'd open up.

Beam weapons started buzzing and Heat instinctually ducked but the action wasn't taking place in their module. In fact, it was happening on the other side. Had they started fighting amongst themselves? Without scans, he couldn't tell for sure but it would make sense based on what Fielding told him about the pirate's message.

A marine fired at the front of the line. Heat clenched his weapon tighter, trying to see what happened but the corridor was too narrow. "Report! What's going on?" The station shook and air hissed for a moment before a loud clatter resounded through the module. "What the hell is going on?"

"Hendricks fired on us!" Vine shouted. "He's . . . He's gone!"

"Clear the Goddamn way!" Heat shoved them forward, stepping into the module. The door leading to the shuttle was down, cutting off the short hallway that led to their ship. Hendricks and the other guy, Stellen, were gone. The others gathered around. "Okay, what the hell? Gillet, form a perimeter. What did you see, Vine? What happened?"

"We came in . . . Our own guys fired at us. Stellen dashed down the hall . . . He started shooting . . ." Vine shook his head. "Hendricks followed him and the shuttle disconnected from the station. The airlock closed and . . . they're gone!"

"Jesus Christ." Heat turned away, motioning to the doors. "No one comes through those! Keep them *locked down*." He got on the com. "Fielding, we have a serious problem! We haven't encountered team two yet and our shuttle just became dislodged from the station. Two men went with it. Do you see them? Are they okay?"

"Stand by," Fielding said. Heat forced himself not to pace, especially as the screams from other rooms grew more intense. The weapon fire remained in the beam variety but only a few moments passed before their own type of rifles started going off, the report of projectiles adding to the chaos and mess.

"Lieutenant . . ." Heat said. "We're getting pretty damn short on time here, sir."

"We have the shuttle," Fielding said. "But they're not responding to com messages. They've engaged the engines so there might be a problem. I don't see your men. I'm having the fighters do a pass to find out. Also . . . more bad news, I can't raise team two or their shuttle. You're on your own for a moment but I'd make my way to the other ship. It's still docked."

"But you can't raise them," Heat said. "Okay, we'll head that way."

"Gunny!" Vine shouted. "I think we're about to have incoming!"

"You heard what I said," Heat replied. "It moves, you kill it. I want you to all remain focused. Listen to me, follow orders and we'll get through this. No mistakes. We're in this for keeps, gentlemen."

"Heat," Gillet said. "You heard those guns too. That's team two . . . and if they're not answering coms, they might have had the same problem that Hendricks and Stellen had."

"Which is what, exactly?" Heat demanded.

"That's the problem. We don't know and there's no real way to find out easily."

"What do you propose?" Heat asked. "Because I'm not seeing a lot of options here. We're going to have to get through them, find a way off this place. If the Orb's here, we'll need another way to get it."

"I don't . . . really know." Gillet paused. "I . . . I don't even know why I brought that up. It was like . . . I was just looking for an argument."

Heat recognized it. The way his friend acted, it made sense. That's what happened to the pirate's people. "We have to stay focused. Just follow my lead." He pointed at the door. "We're going to go through there and kill whatever's in our way. Hopefully, team two is still on our side. Alright, I'm first one out the door. Here we go!"

Heat stepped up to the entrance to the next module and the door slid open. A firefight raged within, two sides blasting away. He immediately recognized the uniform of four Tol'An operatives, shooting it out with five more of the Pahxin technicians. He was about to order an attack when a third group came in through another door.

The newcomers were dressed in tattered rags, carrying makeshift melee weapons. They descended upon the technicians, battering their skulls and taking them to the ground. As their victims fell, they dropped on top of them, ripping at their flesh with bare hands and knives. The display looked like something out of a horror vid.

The Tol'An didn't hesitate, they turned to Heat's men and started to lift their weapons.

"Light them up!" Heat shouted, firing his own weapon. They riddled their targets with bullets, making them dance back against the wall. When they finished, he turned, noting that the guys with the melee weapons were gone . . . along with the bodies they'd attacked. "Are you kidding me? Did anyone see them go?"

"I missed it," Gillet said.

"Doesn't matter." Heat plunged on toward the shuttle. "Let's just keep moving. I'm sure we'll find those guys when we have to. Hopefully, they just knew their weapons wouldn't work on us."

But he saw the way they looked when they attacked their prey. They had a specific task in mind and would be back. Of that, he was certain. The key was to be gone long before that confrontation could take place . . . and they had to find out just how tough a bunch of psychotic freaks with clubs could be.

Chapter 6

Cassie rubbed her eyes hard as a sudden headache struck. It washed over her the moment she performed another system sensor sweep while waiting for the next audio file to prepare. When she opened her eyes, she gasped, recoiling into her seat with enough force to make it squeak.

"Cassie?" Salina said. "What's wrong? Are you okay?"

The muffled voice became a peripheral sound on the edge of her awareness. Cassie typed furiously, trying to capture what she saw. Beyond the ship, far out beside the station, debris floated about the area, a boneyard of vessels and natural rubble. Life signs littered the entire station, hundreds of them moving about.

"Hey!" Salina snapped her fingers next to her. "Can you hear me? What happened?"

Cassie felt Vincent and Desmond come close as well. She recognized their concern, each of them leaning to look at what she saw.

"Um . . ." Vincent spoke up. "What're we looking at?"

"The scan . . ." She pointed at the screen. "There's . . . Look!"

Salina moved over, peering over her shoulder. "I don't see anything. It's the same nothing we've been looking at."

"No!" Cassie gestured again then tapped her controls to bring it up on the main screen. "Look! There are hundreds of people on the station! Destroyed ships, debris, rubble! Look!"

They all complied, turning to peer at the big screen. Desmond exchanged a concerned look with Vincent but before they could speak, Salina held up her hand.

"Before we judge this, remember what the marines just located." Salina motioned to her own station. "I haven't been able to find anything but what she's describing sounds far more accurate to what we would've expected. Especially after her little pirate broadcast. Which would mean something is not jamming our scans at all."

"What're you suggesting?" Desmond asked. "What do you think is happening then?"

Cassie stood up. "I know." She got on the com, patching into Gil. "Can you please report to the bridge right away?" Turning to the others, she composed herself with a deep breath. "I had contact with the Orb. It took a bit, pressing and finding out about these pirates but I think that's why I can see the truth now."

"Whatever it is," Salina said, "is blocking our minds. Making us see specifically what it wants us to see . . . Which, in this case, is nothing."

"Luring us in," Desmond replied. "Offering us a false sense of security so we'd board the facility." He looked sharply at Vincent. "And get close. Zach! Full reverse. Get us well away from that station. Vincent, get Fielding to have those marines extract right away. If what Cassie described is happening, they're in over their heads."

Gil stepped onto the bridge, his expression grave. "I suppose I will not be going to the station then?"

"Come look at my screen!" Cassie pointed. "Quick!"

Gil joined her, leaning to peer at it. "My apologies, I've been suffering from . . . a . . . severe . . . headache. What am I looking at? I thought this sector was clear. Totally empty. That was part of the mystery I hoped to solve." He turned back to Cassie. "What's happened? Where did all that come from?"

"Think through it," Cassie said. "You and I are the only ones who are seeing this on the bridge."

"Oh my." Gil stepped closer to the captain. "Are we putting distance between us and the station?"

"We are."

"I wonder if this is somehow contagious." Gil rubbed his chin. "We would need samples from the station to find out. Air, blood from those exposed to it . . . perhaps even from the metal walls themselves. But I'm guessing that won't be happening. Do we know if the marines have acted peculiar?"

"Fielding's having a hard time with communications," Vincent said. "I reached out to have the marines return to the ship as soon as possible but he wasn't able to raise them on hails."

"Shit." Desmond scowled. "Have the pilots try. They're in close proximity. We need to check in with them anyway. See if they're having any problems. Being right there might've triggered something. Thank you, Cassie. Keep at those audio files. Gil, help her. I want to know how that played out."

"This doesn't make sense though," Salina said. "Why wouldn't our pilots have run into all that stuff out there? How would they be able to pass right through unscathed? They would've bumped into *something*. The statistics of them avoiding it all without seeing it are astronomical. Not even worth calculating."

Gil answered, "whatever this is likely is keeping them alive. This type of manipulation could range from extremely subtle to overt. If this force can blind us to the reality of the situation, think of what else it might push on us? No, what we're faced with here is utterly fascinating. Certainly, the most potent thing I've encountered in many years."

"Glad to have impressed you," Desmond said. "I think we can get back to work now, folks. We'll have time to theorize later. I want everyone safe *then* we'll decide what to do next."

***

Dulain arrived at Reach's office, knocking twice before entering. The admiral looked up, his face strained from stress. According to reports from his subordinates, he hadn't been sleeping well and it was starting to show. Eventually, he'd need some downtime and the AIA was prepared to help him realize it.

Until then, they needed to collaborate and keep the machine moving.

"I'm just here to give you a quick update," Dulain said. "Two of our operatives are infiltrating a base in Eastern Europe. Marines cleared it out a few years ago but apparently, someone's decided it was too good of a place to ignore. They might not be there anymore, but we figure we can grab some evidence."

"And you think these might be the traitors you're tracking?"

"Evidence supports they might be using this location," Dulain replied. He took a seat. "We'll know soon. I sent Christina to investigate."

"Seems rash," Reach said, "sending your lead agents on such a mission. Surely, you have other people more suitable."

"Maybe, but not better." Dulain shrugged. "She's going to find what we need out there if there's anything to find. And if not, she'll be back soon. My instincts tell me we're going to find something though and get closer to catching the people who are undermining our efforts. Then, we can unleash the military."

"That promise was rather bold, I admit."

Dulain smiled. "Yes, Christina wasn't happy about it but I understand the purpose. It gives us the opportunity to keep everyone involved. They don't like being kept in the dark any more than we do. Unfortunately, once intelligence turns things over to our militant friends, we tend to be cast aside. We have to be sure before we step away."

"Understood. Thank you for working so closely with us. It's a refreshing change from when you were spying on me."

Dulain wondered when that would come up again. He wasn't surprised. Reach made it clear how sore he was about Christina being planted with him but even after a couple good venting sessions, he remained vocal about his dissatisfaction. There wasn't much to be done about it other than to apologize again.

"You were in the midst of something we needed in on with unfettered intelligence," Dulain explained again. "It wasn't personal and honestly, it worked out. She saved your life when you were captured after all. I'd say it was a good thing, even if you didn't necessarily like what it meant."

"Yes, well . . . it's just refreshing to all be working together as we should've been."

"I take full responsibility for that decision," Dulain said. "But I won't apologize again. I think we're past that now. It's time to move on. In fact." He checked his watch. "I need to get up to operations. I want to know the second Christina's mission is complete. We might have to take immediate action, after all."

"Keep me informed," Reach said. "We'll talk later."

"Indeed." Dulain left the room, walking casually toward the control center. There would be no news for hours but that didn't stop him from wanting to be out of the admiral's presence. They'd been working well together but there were limits to their tolerance of one another. The past wasn't kind to either of them for various reasons.

But at least we're making progress, Dulain thought. *No one can argue our results*.

***

Alicia allowed her fighter to drift, on her patrol pattern, sitting to take in her surroundings. She figured space would be desolate, empty . . . perhaps even boring at times but she never expected such an absolute wasteland. How did the previous inhabitants bring about such a state? Did they have incredible recycling? Cleaning crews?

Who cares? Alicia sighed. They didn't need fighters on that mission, they needed the shuttles. They could've flown around and gathered data, proving the place was empty. Those larger vessels had better scanning equipment anyway. But command worried about aerial engagements so . . . Charger and Mustang scrambled.

I keep hearing this is probably the last mission we'll run without an attack force, Alicia thought. *I can't believe it's going to be a milk run that ends with us falling asleep behind the flight sticks.*

"All pilots," Dennis's voice broke through the boredom for a moment. "I have some bad news. Command has just reported that we need to return to the Gnosis immediately. Make your way back as quickly as possible. Follow the course I'm sending to your computers to avoid any collisions."

"What?" Alicia didn't bother to hide her skepticism. "What are you talking about? Collision with what? Open space? Come on, sir. This place is empty."

"Not according to the report," Dennis insisted. "We'll take up your concern when we arrive back at the ship, Flight Lieutenant. Now move!"

Alicia shook her head, altering course to follow the odd line Dennis put up on the monitor. It was erratic, moving very much like they were going through an invisible obstacle course. *Maybe this is just a test*, she thought. *What else makes sense? That solid debris and obstacles are actually invisible?*

But hadn't they encountered plenty of strange things already? *Command wouldn't throw this out if it wasn't necessary*. She started along the path, matching the recommended speed when her scanner went crazy. Blips appeared, not even a thousand kilometers behind her from the other side of the station.

"Um . . . you guys seeing this?" Alicia asked. "I've got contact."

"Negative I . . ." Dennis stopped mid-sentence. "Holy crap. Those are on an intercept course!"

Alicia took a breath to reply when the world around her seemed to shimmer. Rocks, chunks of metal the size of small buildings appeared, winking into existence. It took every ounce of discipline she could muster not to react, jerking her flight stick to compensate for the sudden perception of being surrounded.

The com channel lit up with shock as the other pilots must've suddenly seen what they were supposed to avoid as well. *I'll never question command on their crazy again*, Alicia thought, veering to clear the debris field. She hit her afterburners, putting distance between her and the boneyard before turning her attention to the incoming fighters.

"Are we engaging?" Alicia asked.

"Trying to hail them now," Dennis said. "But they're not answering on any com network. These ships don't look like any we've encountered before. Not Kalrawv or Tol'An . . . not Pahxin. What the hell are they?"

Commander Bowman came on the line. "Gil states that these ships you're seeing commonly belong to scavengers. They likely fell victim to whatever you're seeing out there because they are *not* responding to any coms at all. However, we're picking up an energy spike consistent with weapon systems. You are free to attack."

Works for me. Alicia acquired a target though it was still out of range. Dennis gave them the go order as well as they formed up on one another. Racing to meet the attackers, scans gave them a good readout of what to expect: missiles and beam weapons. The heavier ordnance rode outside, on the bottoms of the ships.

Shields remained on par with Tol'An designs, but not as good as what the Earth ships packed. Their research and partnership with the Pahxin paid off, giving them a defensive advantage. *That's all well and good, but why are these guys attacking us at all? Are they trying to defend their claim?* Distance to target began to plunge, numbers spinning on the HUD. Alicia doubled her front shields. Enemy ships opened fire, beams cutting through the dark of space. They didn't seem to be aiming, their attacks lacking any sort of consistent trajectory. Even their formation suffered as their ships hopped out like the pilots were shaking the flight sticks violently.

Dennis came up beside Alicia, dodging quickly away when a series of blasts came between them. It was the first time the enemy ships actually tried to connect with them. She closed within range, firing energy weapons at her first target. It veered wildly out of the way, a dramatic overcompensation that nearly made it collide with one of its allies.

"What the hell?" Alicia dove to avoid another attack, performing a barrel roll before climbing sharply. She came around behind an enemy ship and blasted him, tearing through the shields. Chunks of metal broke free as the thrusters went dark. She switched to projectiles, perforating the fuselage of her target.

The fighter went up but the pilot seemed to make no effort to eject.

Um . . . what is wrong with these people?

Two beams struck her on the side, absorbed by her shields. Alicia turned to meet them, heading straight for them. She'd hoped to intimidate them but instead, they picked up speed and stopped firing. *They're going to ram me . . . That's definitely the look of someone who plans to ram me.*

Alicia dropped the game of chicken, hitting her top thrusters to send her out of their range. They didn't bother to follow, instead fixating on their next potential target. One of them clipped a Charger fighter, catching them on the side. Both went spinning out of control but the Earth ship managed to recover.

The scavenger vessel slammed into the station, exploding in a spectacular fashion. When the globular flames cleared, a jagged hole was left behind, cascading debris from the station into space before some automated emergency system erected a force field. Half the station could've become decompressed in that short time.

I hope the marines are okay. Another attacker came upon her, firing away before darting off. He didn't even seem interested in following up, rather he continued on a new course out of the conflict altogether. *Is he fleeing? Repositioning? These pilots are completely insane! There's no rhyme or reason to their tactics.*

Scans showed more fighters coming in but this time, the silhouettes were very familiar. Tol'An, ready to get into the action. But who would they attack? The scavengers? Mustang? Alicia wondered how insane they would be and if the affliction was something to worry about. She jammed her afterburners to full, taking herself well out of the action for a moment.

"We have more incoming," Alicia said. "Looks like . . . six Tol'An vessels on intercept course." She looked about the environment, trying to decide the best course of action. The debris field was not too far off from where the other fighters did battle. The erratic flight patterns might even be used to their advantage.

She ran a quick scan of the area, noting that it was not as dense as she initially thought. "I've got an idea," Alicia called to the others. "Um . . . hold tight while I give this a try."

"What're you doing?" Dennis asked. "Don't do something insane, Alicia. I'm serious."

"It's not too insane," Alicia replied. "Besides, it'll buy you some breathing room, which you very well might need if they decide to close in on the Gnosis." She tapped the computer, setting waypoints so she could follow them into the debris field then . . . she sent herself hurtling toward the nearest enemy fighters.

Just gotta get your attention, Alicia thought. *Then we'll see if you can clear your heads long enough to survive a little fancy flying.*

***

Fielding struggled to get ahold of the marines but through the static, only screams were audible in the static. Strange war cries and horror peeked through, chilling his blood each time it became more distinct. The computer couldn't translate the words, but they weren't merely inarticulate sounds. There were distinct syllables, each horrifying and rough.

What the hell am I even hearing?

Camera feeds also died.

"Fielding," Vincent's voice made him jump, "we've got a lot going on suddenly. Have you been able to reach the marines yet?"

"Negative," Fielding replied. "Maybe we should go out there and get them."

"Under no circumstances will anyone be going to that station now," Vincent said. "We can't trust our eyes. I'm about to have the doctor start looking into what's going on. It's a miracle we're not having more problems over here. Have you been able to reach the shuttles? They're not responding to hails either."

"No, and the last contact I had was with team one. Team two dropped off shortly after they arrived at the station proper." Fielding sighed. "So what is happening, Commander? What are we not seeing?"

"A debris field, for one," Vincent replied. "Couple that with God knows what on the station . . . At least a hundred life forms, maybe more. We didn't pick any of that up when we first arrived so there you go. Welcome to the unknown part of our investigations, huh?"

"Before I lost contact, team one was forced to kill some of the Pahxin technicians. They were attacked . . . and their opponents wouldn't stand down, wouldn't surrender." Fielding paused for a moment. "Do you think this problem might . . . I don't know . . . impact behavior?"

"The dogfighting I'm seeing would indicate yes. The enemy pilots have no regard for their personal safety. It's bad, Fielding. Keep trying to reach your people. We have to get them off of there . . . then quarantine them until we know what's happened."

"Understood." That last bit annoyed Fielding but he understood the precaution. They had no idea what those men encountered in the station and if it was some kind of disease, then that would lead to many more lives being risked. He tried again to reach them, shifting channels, working to clean up the signal but he still had no luck.

Sitting back, Fielding ran his hands over his head and as he considered giving up, a long shot came to him. Voice communication was down but maybe he could send a far simpler signal. Their HUDs should be able to interpret Morse code, even if they didn't know it right away. It might be the only way to get through.

Composing a quick message, Fielding set the computer to send it continuously until they received a reply. He followed up with a request to engineering to have a technician look into what might be causing the interference. With any luck, they'd have a response soon. He fought against rising frustration.

Two full teams were at risk over there and if they couldn't be reached, they might all be lost. Fielding couldn't let himself think like that, couldn't indulge the pessimism. Not when there was even a glimmer of hope.

***

Combatants piled into the next module, cutting off the marine's path to the other shuttle. Vine and Anderson took either side of the door. Kelly and Brock crouched with their weapons aimed at the entrance. Erskin and Bosh guarded their rear. Gillet stood ready to support either side.

Heat tried to get through to the Gnosis again, reaching out to Fielding. More static. His head started aching just before he found the blood and it finally started to lighten up. None of the others complained about the pain. An epiphany struck him, a thought about the Orb. It must've had something to do with it.

My contact with it . . . That insane vision it gave me . . . That's what drew me to the blood and the recording. Heat wondered if it would help him anymore. *Anything would be welcome at this point. Knowing my luck, my next inspiration will draw us directly into the middle of some enemy camp on this godforsaken facility.*

People on the other side of the door began chanting, some kind of staccato war cry that grew in volume and intensity. They started speaking, escalated to shouts them screamed until they made inarticulate noise. Heat looked at Gillet, feeling at a loss for words. The enemy's sounds must've been meant to intimidate and it started working, at least on Bosh.

"Maybe we should fall back," Bosh offered. "I'm sure we could find a way around them."

"We stand here," Heat said. "We'll finish them and push on. There's no time to dally with the shuttle. We have to get there or we're done. Do you all get me? Stay focused. When that door opens, you fire and you do *not* let them get very far. This module is our home and they're about to invade it. Don't tell me any of you are okay with them coming into your territory."

The men shouted their agreement, a brief cry of solidarity. Heat hoped it would be enough to keep their morale until they finished the fight. If those on the other side of the door held clubs and blades, the fight would be easy. If they were armed with beam weapons, it held a certain amount of danger.

But one way or another, Heat and his men were going that way and nothing in that station would stop them.

The doors burst open. Shouts filled the air. Men flooded into the room, carrying melee weapons as they'd seen before. Four of the marines immediately opened fire, tearing through the front line of their attackers. Bodies hit the ground, pieces of flesh and clothes splattered the wall or hovered briefly before slapping the floor.

Heat had no idea how many they killed before the next wave approached, this one using beam weapons. They only barely started to fire when the whole station shook violently. Heat lost his balance, slamming his back against the wall. The others stumbled but kept their footing. Hostilities were temporarily halted when the lights flickered.

Holy God, this is insane! Heat checked his HUD, thanking whatever divine power had his back for the fact that his scans were working. Something collided with the station, tearing a hole in the hull seven modules away. Automated maintenance kicked in, dropping a force field in place but that section of the station lost all compression.

Oxygen levels started to rise, albeit slowly. *We'd be okay in the armor*, Heat thought, *but these maniacs running around would've died instantly*.

As if on cue to his thoughts, the beams lit up again. Marines moved to take cover, returning fire. The doors opened beside Heat and a man slipped in, carrying a makeshift blade out of sharpened shards of metal. He lifted it over his head and charged. Heat hit him in the face with the butt of his weapon, knocking the man instantly unconscious.

I need this guy alive. Heat turned to Gillet. "We have to fall back. Bring this guy with us."

"Why? He looks dead!"

"I knocked him out and I've got questions!" Heat simmered for half a moment before regaining full control of himself. "Listen, we don't have time to argue. We're bringing him, we're falling back, we're learning more about the situation. Guys! Fall back, two at a time, cover fire! We're locking down the next module!"

It was clear Vine wanted to argue but he had to stop when he took a blast to the leg. Crying out, he stumbled back but it looked like he was no worse the wear. A black scorch marked the front of his thigh and that was the extent of the damage. No melting, no corrosion. He fell back with the others.

Gillet grabbed the downed captive and they escaped to the next room, just as the others surged forward. They were rewarded with a final barrage of bullets before the doors closed, giving them another moment of respite. "Lock those down!" Heat barked. "And give me some space. I want to know how these assholes got here . . . and what happened specifically."

Chapter 7

Christina crouched behind a low console as bullets glanced off the wall six inches above her head. She reloaded her weapon, thinking back to the brief moment not even twenty minutes earlier when their mission moved from stealth operation to full on loud firefight with an unknown number of men.

They found the base, nestled neatly between two peaks in the middle of the mountains. Scans indicated it was deserted but their first glimpse told them that was wrong. Guards stood at the top of the building, staring out in four directions and dim lights reflected out of the windows.

How did we miss those from aerial? Christina wondered about their methods for collecting intel. *If I survive this, I'm running them through the paces to figure out what happened specifically.*

The base itself sported walls on the sides flanked by mountains, which were attached to the base spanning across from one side to the next. Three buildings extended two stories down and three up. Scans indicated the walls were electrified with doors providing access to the various paths around the area, likely for scouting patrols.

They didn't encounter any people on their descent but when they arrived, there was a man standing outside. He lingered around a solid metal door, staring off to the left. Christina took aim, engaging the silencer on her submachine gun. Clicking it to single fire mode, she zeroed in on his head and depressed the trigger.

The gun whisper-clicked and the man jerked in place before collapsing to the ground. Christina and Essex dashed forward, right up to the door. They obscured the body with some snow before she began to hack into the security system. "Cover me." She turned to her tablet while her partner stood guard.

Wind picked up, blowing snow all about them. Weather reports suggested they didn't have to worry about snow but mountains didn't always cooperate with meteorology. When the cool breeze buffeted her back, she sensed a change. It worried her because if a storm came up, if it escalated, the shuttle might not be able to pull off a clean extract.

We'd be stuck down here with God knows how many enemies? Christina stepped back as the door opened. "We're in."

"Thank God," Essex muttered. "It's cold as a witch's tit out here."

"Charming." Christina directed him to go first. "I'll get the door."

Once the door closed and the wind stopped, they found themselves in an eerily silent chamber. The change in temperature made her start to sweat. Each of them surveyed their surroundings. It was a guard room, complete with locked up weapons and security terminals hooked into cameras all throughout the base.

"This could be useful," Essex said. "Maybe grab personnel data? Find what we're looking for right from here?"

Christina looked over the computer, scanned it with her tablet. She shook her head. "These are dummy stations. They have access to the cameras but no elevated permissions. Their network access is restricted at the hardware level. We're going to have to make our way to their control room."

"And what are we looking for there?"

"Intel," Christina replied. "Whether it be personnel files, communiques or full on military plans. It really depends on how sloppy they were with their security. I've seen people make some insanely bad decisions before. However . . ." She tapped a button on the terminal and brought up a different set of cameras on the screens. "We've got some things to get through."

The courtyard beyond the guard station showed at least four men walking around. They seemed to be on some sort of security rotation but they didn't just move back and forth. Each of them zigged and zagged in the open, crossing paths and acknowledging one another. Taking them out would've required popping all of them at once.

Impractical to say the least.

"How're we going to slip through?" Essex asked. "Do you want to go out shooting? We've got suppressors."

"No," Christina said. "We're good shots, but I don't want to risk a miss. We've got to be smart about this. When we go out, we'll take a hard right and go to the wall. Wait for them to cross at the middle and run. If we're at all lucky, we'll reach the next building before we're seen. If not . . ." She sighed. "I guess we shoot them and hope for the best."

"That sounds fine to me." Essex stepped over to the door leading into the courtyard. "You want me to take point?"

"Not this time," Christina replied. "Follow my lead, please. I'll get us out there and to the wall. Then, sprint like hell, okay?" She sized him up. "I'm guessing you're a little faster than I am. Don't knock me over when you start moving. Whoever gets to the wall first will turn around and cover the other person in the event that we're seen. Got it?"

"I'm in."

Christina watched the screen until the men met at the middle. She opened the door and slipped out, moving swiftly toward the end of the building. They arrived at the wall, pressed into the corner. It should've been a reasonable blind spot but she didn't want to risk it for long. The two of them crouched there, allowing the patrol to reach the extent of their perimeter.

The men moved back toward one another, starting another rotation. This time, they broadened their pattern, staying closer to the walls. Christina noticed they were each hugging themselves, slapping their arms and stomping their feet as they walked. She figured they must've been out there for at least the better part of an hour.

And they're probably pretty miserable as a result. Miserable people made mistakes, they didn't pay close attention. That meant the next part of the plan should work. As soon as the four individuals returned toward their center, Christina made a quick dash for the next building, sprinting as fast as her legs would carry her.

To her right, the frosty metal wall extended some twelve feet above her while the guards and open courtyard sat to her left. Their destination, the next building, was a mere forty feet ahead. Her legs and lungs began to ache. Adrenaline made her vision blur. Heavy breathing sounded in her ears, competing with the pounding of her heart.

Christina reached the wall, sliding on her knees into cover. She spun, aiming her weapon while Essex caught up. He passed her by, slowing to a walk. A side door provided access another fifty yards down, a secure passage the soldiers might've used back when a real army held the place.

This group was squatting. They probably didn't know all the ways in and out. How long did they intend to stay and more importantly, when did they plan to leave? Where would they go? These were the questions that needed answering before they left the facility. And if there was a storm, they might have plenty of time to search.

Providing they weren't discovered.

Slipping into the larger structure proved no more difficult than the first door, though it opened far slower from lack of use. The cold and years were not particularly kind to the facility, a fact that was made all the more obvious by the state of the first room they entered. Frost clung to the walls, and the empty shelves were covered in rust.

Did they upgrade the technology? If this room is in such a state, then nothing should've worked from the time when the actual military used it.

They crept into a dark hallway. Broken light fixtures lined the walls, up to a single door that happened to be blessedly free of frost. Christina did a scan, showing Essex that there were people on the other side. *We've found the part of the base they're actually using.* She checked and the door was unlocked. *And they don't think anyone can get in this way.*

Moving inside, they found themselves in a large room filled with banks of computers and cables draped across the floor. Most of it was brand new but a few built in consoles were in use. Christina counted fifteen people milling about, all working at different stations throughout the room.

Their low chatter masked the sound of the door opening and none of them even looked in that direction. *This probably has what we need,* Christina thought. *But there's no way we're blending in here.* Two exits presented themselves. Less people stood near the room to the right but that might've meant the left held more valuable, actionable intel.

Christina ultimately elected to go to the right. They slipped through the next door and found themselves in a dark space full of whirring computers. *This is a server room. Jackpot!* She headed left, moving close to one of the nearby consoles. "Hey," she whispered. "I'm pretty sure this is exactly what we need. Keep an eye on the door."

"What do I do if someone comes in?"

"Hope they don't have a flashlight," Christina replied. Their helmets provided them with night vision and she could easily see the panel she needed to remove. Whoever built the boxes used a tool-less design, allowing her to remove the section without a screwdriver. It revealed all the internals and a place to plug in.

She fished a dongle from her belt and plugged her tablet in, ordering it to download all the data available. A meter appeared, showing her it would take seven minutes to finish. *Oh my God! That's an eternity!*

"What's wrong?" Essex asked. "You just went stiff."

"The initial estimated time to download this stuff is long," Christina replied. "I'm hoping it's wrong and goes down. Even if it doesn't though, I'd say we scored big. Providing we can get it out of here, we'll probably have everything we need about these guys."

Why would it take so long if you're hard wired in?" Essex shook his head. "It seems fishy."

"I think it's just a ton of data." Christina hummed. Even as she said it, she began to doubt. She had to remind herself of Occam's Razor: the simplest explanation tended to be the correct one. Poorly optimized, large data sets made more sense than these people having some kind of amazing security tech in place.

After all, they didn't even bar the outside doors nor did they guard large sections of the facility.

It took forever, but the data did finish downloading after nearly ten minutes. No one even peeked their heads inside to look around. The server room appeared to be both off limits and a place without cameras. Christina checked, noting another door on the far side of the room.

She elected to try that one instead of going back the way they came. Chances were good someone would be standing around out there and she didn't want to risk it. Heading across the space and performed a quick scan. One person showed up on the far left nearly sixty yards away.

They stepped through the door and went to the right, heading for another hallway.

Christina rounded the corner but Essex was a few feet behind her. "Hey!" A voice sounded from the end of the hall, making Christina's stomach drop. "What're you doing there? What's going on?"

Essex took aim and fired, putting a round in the man's face at fifty yards. The body hit the deck, making a clang sound on the metal grating. Doors opened at the end of the hall as people came out to see what happened. Christina grabbed Essex and they hurried off, trying to make it back toward the unused part of the base.

As they came to the next door, it opened before they could get there and three men stepped out. Each of them expressed shock at seeing the two spies and Christina opened up, throwing a couple quick bursts into them. Their bodies danced backward, hitting the walls before dropping dead.

An alarm went off.

"Shit." Christina sighed, tapping her com. She reached out to the shuttle. "We need an immediate evac. Give me a good location to meet you."

"I'm two minutes out," the pilot said. "Did you just alert the base?"

"Affirmative," Christina said. "Hurry up. I don't have time to tell you a story. Where can you get us?"

"They have anti-aircraft down there. You'll have to get to the coordinates I just sent you. Half a mile from the base."

"God damn it." Christina clenched her fist but she didn't argue. "Okay. We'll see you soon. Don't leave without us." She motioned for Essex to follow her. "This is where the rest of our trip gets damn exciting. I hope you're ready."

"Shouldn't be too much of a problem," Essex said. "They're not ready for what we've got to throw at them."

Christina really wanted to argue that with him but it wasn't the time. She led him out through the next room and toward their escape route, the abandoned part of the base. The door opened and they stepped into the hallway with the broken light fixtures. Guns went off, bullets slapping the walls all around them.

Essex returned fire. Things went into chaos. They started running, driven away from their planned route. Deeper into the base they fled, engaging in a running gun battle. Essex took a grazing shot to the arm. Christina's helmet got a nick from a particularly lucky shot but they got into a reactor area where they could take cover behind the low protective rails. Christina reloaded her weapon as someone fired at her, putting rounds into the wall just opposite the catwalk. She leaned out and shot back, counting five people closing on their position. "Change of plan," she used the com to reach their pilot. "I'm going to need you to risk those anti-aircraft guns."

"Are you insane?" He asked. "If I get shot down in there, then we're all dead!"

"If you don't try, then we're likely not going to make it out of here," Christina said. "And believe me, the information I have in this tablet is worth the risk. Now get your ass moving. Stay low and they'll have a hard time targeting you. Once you're close, we'll come out and we can make a running extract. Copy?"

"Copy," the pilot grumbled, sounding incredibly pissed. "Just be ready, agent. This sounds insane."

"That's kind of our job description," Christina replied. "Yours included. I'll keep the line hot." She shouted to Essex. "You still okay?"

Another bunch of gunfire blasted the walkway beside her, slapping the wall again. It made her stay put in her cover.

Essex stood and fired several long bursts before returning to his own cover. "I'm good! Reloading!" He dropped the magazine and slapped another one in.

"Cease fire!" shouted one of the attackers, and the shooting did indeed stop. He spoke with a Slavic accent though Christina couldn't immediately place the region of origin. "You're both surrounded. There is no way out. Whatever you hoped to achieve in breaking in has failed. Surrender! Or you'll be killed."

Christina checked for the shuttle's location. He was still a good minute out. *Time to stall.* "What're you doing here?" She called back. "This isn't exactly a vacation spot and the people who built it took off years ago. Care to explain?"

"That is none of your concern! Are you here to investigate our secrets?"

"We just got lost and thought we'd take a look around," Christina replied. "If it's all the same to you, we'd like to go out the way we came in. We can let bygones be bygones. You know. Water under the bridge or whatever. Just . . . step back and let us go. I promise we won't tell anyone about you squatting here."

"I want to know who you work for! Surrender!"

Damn, he's getting forceful. Christina noted the shuttle would be there in less than thirty seconds. They'd have to get to the edge of the base to board the thing and that meant giving the enemy a decent target to shoot at. Then she remembered all the grenades Essex brought. She turned to him and motioned toward his belt.

"We'll probably need those in a second," Christina said. "When we make a break for it."

"Understood."

"I'll tell you what," Christina shouted. "We're going to think about your surrender option for a moment. Is that okay? Decide how badly we want to live? Can you give us that time?"

"No!" The man grunted before continuing. "I don't know what game you're trying to play with me here but I'm not having it! Throw down your weapons *right now* and come out! I will not ask again! In fact . . ." He lowered his voice, giving orders to the men around him. "My men are coming to confiscate your equipment."

The rumble of the shuttle engine sounded overhead. Half a moment later, an explosion shook the ground followed by another. Christina held her breath, praying she'd just heard the destruction of the anti-aircraft guns rather than their ride but when the thrusters engaged, relief washed through her.

"Throw those grenades," Christina said. "Let's get the hell out of here!"

Essex tossed two grenades and immediately primed two more. They went sailing through the air, bouncing on the metal before exploding seconds later. People screamed. Others ran. The explosions helped foster chaos. Christina led the way toward the courtyard, firing her weapon to suppress the enemies nearby.

They got out in the open, near the taller buildings. The shuttle's turrets blasted away, swiveling about as it drove back hordes of enemy soldiers. "We're on our way!" Christina shouted. "Get the back open! Now!"

The shuttle spun around and dropped the ramp. Beam weapons started tearing through the air, a clear indication that this particular enemy had a benefactor beyond anyone on Earth. Christina felt something hot graze her left leg and it almost took her down. Essex cried out. She glanced back, but he was still moving.

They arrived at the shuttle. Christina jumped, dragging herself inside before turning to help Essex. He grabbed her hand, straining to hoist himself inside. Once his upper half was in and only his legs dangled out, she turned to tell the pilot to go. A strong hand grabbed her leg, threatening to yank her out.

She grabbed the safety handle of the shuttle and clung to it just as one of the enemies pulled himself up and into the shuttle.

"Go!" Christina shouted, rolling to her feet. The invader, a tall man with curly black hair and several days of facial hair, looked like a beast. His uniform was unkempt, wrinkled and wet from the snow. He didn't have any weapons, just his balled fists and a wild look in his eyes. He advanced.

Christina lifted her weapon but he threw a circle kick, knocking it out of her hand. The sling kept it attached to her body. Before she could recover from the attack, he danced forward and threw a punch, connecting with her jaw and neck. Had the gun not pulled her off balance, he might've broken a bone. Pain lit up her senses but it didn't slow her down.

She retaliated, not giving him a moment to think he'd made progress. Leading with a thrust kick, he dodged to the right. His retaliation came from another punch but this time, she was prepared and ducked, coming back up with his arm over her shoulders. He stood on her left. She grabbed his fist with her left hand, holding him in place.

He tried to pull away and she let him go, accompanying the motion with a swift elbow to the chin. It knocked him backward onto the ground. Before he could rise, she kicked him on the thigh. He shoved at her legs, driving her back so he could crawl into a crouch. Diving forward, he tried to tackle her but she stepped aside so only one arm went around her waist.

They toppled to the ground and he slid, nearly falling out of the shuttle. Essex grabbed Christina's arm and pulled, keeping her from going out. The man struggled, screaming at the top of his lungs. Christina drew her free leg back and kicked him in the face, pounding him three times before his grip finally loosened.

Blood matted his beard, his eyes swelled shut but he still clung to her, however loosely. A final blow from her boot sent him tumbling out of the shuttle to his death somewhere in the mountains.

"Jesus Christ . . ." Christina slumped back on the floor. "Close the door. It's colder than shit in here."

Essex complied then flopped into one of the chairs. "Is this how it always goes?"

"Nah," Christina said from the floor. "Sometimes it's way worse. Though at this very moment, I'm not sure how. Did you get hurt?"

"Shot to the shoulder," Essex replied. "Seems the tactical armor prevented serious damage. I think it's just burned."

"We'll be back at Gamma Alpha soon enough and they can look at both of us." Christina turned to her tablet and patted it. "Hopefully, we got everything we need to deal with these terrorist assholes because I do *not* want to go through something like that again. Next time someone faces those jerks, it'll be the military."

"They seemed well armed for a faction group," Essex pointed out. "You think they've been outfitted by some other force?"

"I guarantee it." Christina crawled to her feet and sat on one of the chairs, tossing her weapon in the seat beside her. "Now to find out who did it and shut them down. But that's not for us to deal with, Essex. Good job. You definitely had my back out there. I appreciate it."

"I feel like I made a lot of mistakes."

"We'll worry about a full evaluation when we're home and safe." Christina closed her eyes. "For now, I'm going to pretend I don't have this job. Talk to you when we get back, Essex. Thanks again."

Chapter 8

Alicia thought her plan might be partially successful in that she could get two or three enemy ships to follow her. When five of them started chasing, she wondered how she became so popular. Two Tol'An ships and three scavenger vessels pursued her toward the debris field, each one firing erratically while buzzing behind her like insane bees.

"Are you luring them into the field?" Dennis asked. "Alicia, that's insane!"

"So are they," Alicia said. "So I'll be in good company . . . for so long as it takes them to crash and burn."

"Have you thought about the possibility that *you* might crash and burn?"

"Nah, never have considered that as a likely event." Alicia stretched her neck before tilting her head in focus. "If you don't mind, sir, I really need to concentrate for the next few moments so . . . I'll talk to you when I get out on the other side. Quinn out for now." She switched off the com just seconds before entering the boneyard.

One thing about space felt unnatural to Alicia and that involved light. Dropping into a canyon, pulling off wild maneuvers back on Earth for the aerial show, meant plunging into shadow. But things were either visible or not in her new environment and had it not been for her HUD highlighting the debris, it would've blended in completely.

The space station cast a massive shadow over the trashed vessels and rocks, making it feel like flying beneath a black blanket. Her pursuers didn't slow down and their weapons provided the only light in the area. Each time they fired, damaged chunks of metal faded into view momentarily.

Alicia dropped one of her missiles and increased speed, detonating it a few moments later. The explosion stirred up the bits of rock, scattering them into a web. The enemy pilots plunged through them, their shields handling the majority of the damage but the last one collided with a detached bulkhead.

The resulting explosion from his vessel stirred up half the boneyard in that sector, sending the pieces in every direction. Several would hit the station, others would be cast off into deep space to burn up on some planet light years away. It had no impact on Alicia just yet but she had a long way to go.

The first few kilometers were fairly easy. She veered casually around the worst of it and let the shields burn up smaller chunks. The deeper she went, the worse it became until she was in a constant state of motion, dropping below a large rock, veering left to avoid a ship module then spinning around a cluster of old ordnance.

Something whacked her hard enough to make the ship drop a good ten feet and she had to compensate, nursing the thrusters for increased control. Her pursuers struggled. Another one slammed into something and his blip disappeared from her scanner. Another one tried to climb, to depart the hazard but was crushed between two rocks.

Two remained and Alicia had no idea how they survived other than sheer luck. They were flying like total maniacs and yet somehow managed to get that far. She was approaching the end of the boneyard where she'd emerge into open space again. Clicking on her com, she reached out to all available pilots.

"Anyone on this channel still? Cause . . . I kinda need some help."

"Oh, now you need help, huh?" Dennis asked. "I have your position. Looks like two survived your little stunt run."

"Yeah, and no one's more surprised than me," Alicia grunted, pulling up sharply before flipping sideways. The bottom of her ship skimmed a rock, shields flaring so brightly it nearly blinded her. As she came free from the object, she saw open space not even ten seconds away. "I'll admit it. This was a bad idea."

"Thank God it was educational."

Alicia saw the approaching Mustang fighters on her scanner. They'd be there, but it wouldn't be in time to catch the enemy as they came out of the debris field. She'd have to hold them off . . . or at least survive for reinforcements. When none of the obstacles appeared to be big enough to cause real damage, she hit her afterburners.

Tiny sparks appeared all over the hull, bits of debris burning up as she passed through them. Outside, she drew a deep breath and let it out. Sweat made her clothes cling uncomfortably, making her desperately wish the cockpit wasn't so tight around her. Much as she loved flying, this aspect made her miserable.

The enemies came trundling out of the debris field, each redirecting their course to chase her down. One was Tol'An, the other a scavenger. *Interesting. Do they have a temporary truce?* Alicia increased speed but it was obvious they'd have a firing solution shortly. *Okay, time to stop running.*

Dropping speed, she engaged her maneuvering thrusters and spun in place, rocketing back toward the enemy ships. She fired her beam weapons, rapidly depressing the trigger as she approached. One on the left veered away but the Tol'An ship maintained course, returning fire.

Their blasts hit each other, causing shields to react. Alicia's defenses held, the Tol'An's did not. A purple field seemed to crack around the ship, bursting a moment later like shattering glass. Alicia switched to guns, firing a short burst before they passed by one another, blurs in space.

"You hit him," Dennis said. "Looks like there's a fire in the nose but . . . wait. What the hell is he doing?"

Alicia turned sharply to look. The Tol'An vessel attacked the scavenger, attempting to ram him. *What the fresh hell?* The two ships danced around but the pursuer proved to be far more maneuverable. He slammed into his target, connecting with the rear. Both crafts went up in a spectacular display, fading out a moment later.

"That . . . was incredible," Alicia said. "I don't know what to say."

"Form up," Dennis replied. "We're heading back toward the Gnosis to wait for orders. We can have another talk about foolhardy behavior when we're on our way home."

"I look forward to that," Alicia muttered, spinning around to join the formation. Whatever impacted the people near that station pushed them not only to insanity but removed their sense of self-preservation as well. They'd encountered zealots before just never quite like that. Their opponents didn't seem to want to win so much as cause chaos.

A task they managed quite nicely.

***

General Trall went through the Tol'An resources, working through the logistics of an attack on the human planet of Earth. He needed more intelligence, a better understanding of the opposition they might face. Rumor had it there were spies operating on the planet but he didn't have access to them yet.

I need to know what we're facing there. They have several of the Trindishas. That could mean they have considerable defenses, the kind we might not be capable of easily breaching. They already failed in one attack but he believed hubris to be involved that time. This assault would be very different.

Pahxin forces might be there to defend them, meaning they could count on a major battle above the planet. He'd faced his former brothers before in battle and done quite well, so he was less concerned about them. His worry involved the ground forces and the humans' ability to repel them.

"Sir," one of the soldiers stepped into the room and handed him a tablet. "Report on recent operations. We've lost contact with a ship sent off five days ago. I thought you should know."

"Thank you." Trall took it from him, peering down at the information. It was a fast-moving vessel, large enough for twenty men with plenty of cargo space for spoils. The coordinates they were en route to seemed familiar. He couldn't quite place why but doing a crosscheck with other operations instantly brought something up.

The destroyer Ezria sent to collect the Orb went there. He wondered if it had already arrived and if they'd be able to reach it on communications. They needed to know what they were getting into, realize that other Tol'An had gone missing. Without that information, they very well might find themselves in trouble.

Trall stormed into his command center. "I need you to open a channel to the Dormant Star. Now."

"Yes, sir." The officer on duty tapped at his console, trying to send a message. He sighed before turning around. "I'm sorry, sir. It appears they are in hyperspace at the moment. I'm getting no response."

"Perfect." Trall scowled. "What about this smaller ship? The Venture? Raise them."

"We've been trying . . . They haven't responded in days. They're currently listed as missing in action. A rescue operation was planned but Lord Ezria canceled it as too risky."

"I doubt he knew where they were." Trall rubbed his eyes. The Master had great vision for the overall future of the galaxy, for all governments but his grasp of everyday logistics left something to be desired. "Okay . . . I want you to keep trying the Dormant Star. Set up an automated message to let them know we need them to contact us the moment they arrive."

"Understood."

Trall left the room, returning to his office. He wondered if it might be in their best interest to head out to that place himself, with a large enough force to deal with whatever might be out there. If the Pahxin held the area or even the Kalrawv Group, he would need to deal with them decisively.

He sat down and checked the roster of ships currently orbiting the planet. He had his flagship, a battleship stolen from the Pahxin as well as ten destroyers and a number of scouts. If they left right away, they might be able to plot an efficient enough course to save their people and possibly salvage the mission.

Trall hit the com, blasting a general communication to his command staff. "Prepare my shuttle for departure," he said. "I'll be heading to the flagship immediately. Have navigation start plotting a course to these coordinates. I want it efficient, something that will get us there as swiftly as possible. We have men to save."

He didn't wait for a response before clicking it off. They would tend to his things and ensure they were onboard. There wasn't time to lose. He headed out, moving toward the hangar and what he hoped would be a win for his people. Considering what Gizan had done, they needed one desperately.

***

Salina and Doctor Holland worked together to analyze what might be happening on the station. At first glance, it did not appear to be a medical problem but they couldn't be sure without data. Losing contact with the marines meant their access to samples was impossible. Even the shuttles were not responding.

Cassie went through the audio files from the pirates while performing scans. She seemed to be able to pull information still and offered up what data she could while multitasking. Salina found it frustrating that their only pipeline to gather much needed intelligence rested firmly on the shoulders of only two people.

Gil helped by performing scans as well, trying to offer advice while presenting his findings. Though he could also clearly see the scan data, it wasn't all encompassing of the environment they were trying to analyze. Air samples and blood samples would've been ideal. Neither were available.

"We need to get over there," Doctor Holland said. "Much as I don't want to say that and sure as hell am not volunteering, without direct contact, we'll never figure this out."

"Unless it has nothing to do with the oxygen," Gil said. "The technicians who came to restore this station would've brought hazard equipment. They wouldn't have breathed the air nor been exposed to it while they explored the first time. And the marines are in there with their full armor on and we've seen signs of problems."

"That doesn't help," Salina said. "Because eventually, they *did* take those things off. Even with protection, they were tricked. Wait . . ." An epiphany hit her. "Tricked. Almost by an intelligence."

"What're you saying?" Holland asked.

"I'm thinking through this. Some *thing* has done this to the people who boarded the station. We can't tell if it's a contagion but we can start searching for unusual power readings. Something like those disembodied things we encountered at the temple. Remember that?" She looked at Gil. "You were there."

"Yes." Gil nodded. "I should be able to tweak the scanner to find something like that. I'll start now." He tapped away at the console before stepping back. "Oh my . . ."

"What?" Salina frowned at the screen. "You already did it? Did you find something?"

"I did . . . and yes." Gil pointed to the monitor. "You should be able to see this as well."

Salina narrowed her eyes, leaning close. The scanner picked up a low-level vibration impacting the entire station. It cast a field out around the base nearly six hundred yards in all directions. Any ship that docked with it would've been affected. She directed Holland to look at it.

"Would this have an impact on people?" Salina asked. "Even Pahxin?"

Holland nodded immediately. "Yes, it's at a perfect frequency to cause problems with the nervous system. The sort of thing that Agent Alexander described from the pirates may only be one symptom of this type of low-level . . . noise for lack of a better term. Anywhere from mere annoyance to mania."

"Which we've seen in the enemy pilots," Gil pointed out. "However, it doesn't merely end if someone leaves the field."

Holland shook his head. "It would be like coming down from being angry or frustrated. It takes time and before they have the opportunity to shake the symptoms free, they subject themselves to the source again. I would not say that it's permanent . . . but I'd have to study someone who experienced it to know."

"What's this reading?" Salina pointed to an energy spike deep within the station. "Cassie, you should look at this one too."

Cassie joined them. Gil nudged her as she approached, saying, "that looks somewhat familiar to me . . . but different."

"Yeah." Cassie pointed. "That's close to Orb energy but there's something off about it. Something different. Like . . . Like something's overlaid on top. A filter almost."

"Or a cloud," Holland said. "Because you're right. Those signals are exactly what I was reading when we did the experiment only there's something dampening the power."

"That's why I didn't see it when we arrived," Cassie pointed out. "Well . . . one of the reasons at least."

"Something feeding on it," Salina suggested. "Something thriving on the power of the Orb. We need theories. Thoughts. Anything at all that could help them make sense of it." She turned to Gil. "What've you got?"

"If you look at this system, there are two dead planets," Gil said. "They have no life on them at all, zero activity. Without a survey, I'm guessing on the next part, but I'll bet they used to have settlements. I came up with that because of the debris field that we're now able to see. All that rock, the metal . . . the ships."

"You're thinking . . ." Salina nodded. "I see. You think one of the planets was destroyed."

"Yes. Possibly by whatever we're dealing with. It's transferred itself to the station somehow and there it exists, acting as . . . well, your old mythology calls them sirens. Bringing ships and additional people here."

Cassie added, "if that's the case, then whatever it is can't survive on the Orb's power alone."

"No, it must require some sort of living energy," Holland said. "Oh, but this is total conjecture. We're making it up."

"Even if we're off by a little bit," Salina replied, "it sounds plausible. Think about it. A technical crew shows up on the station and immediately goes missing. No one knows what happened to them. The Tol'An show up, they fly erratically when they engage our fighters and they haven't left with their prize. Then there are the scavengers and pirates as well."

Cassie returned to her station and brought up a scan. "Can you guys see this yet? It doesn't matter. I'll explain. Each faction you described, including ours, have been segregated into different parts of the facility. Our people are here," she pointed, "between where our shuttles docked. You can see large clusters in different ones elsewhere here and here."

Gil hummed, eyes narrow. "If this thing came from a planet with dozens of factions, then this would make sense. It would be used to warring entities. That might even be what it feeds on. I wish we could discover its origin specifically. Such a fascinating creature . . . but with the Orb here, I would be willing to bet it is a manifestation of will."

"Contradictory wills," Cassie clarified. "Each intent on some kind of war that eventually destroyed their planet. When the planet was gone, somehow the station survived and now, this anomaly has hovered around the Orb, remaining alive to bring new victims and additional ships here. All to feed itself."

"And our people," Holland turned to the viewscreen, "are right in the thick of it."

"I'll work on the communications," Gil said. "I might be able to assist with getting through the interference."

Cassie sat down. "I've got the next audio file translated. I can read faster than he speaks. It'll only take a moment."

"Guys," Salina said, "just a thought. Would the Orb survive if the station went up?"

Gil took a step back. "As in, you are wondering what would happen if we *destroyed* the station?" He shook his head. "We might well destroy ourselves. If the Orb exploded, if its energy was released, we would all be dead. There'd be no outrunning it either. I would say that's not even a last resort here."

"Just checking," Salina replied. "Okay, we've got some work to do. Maybe we can find a way to cancel out these vibrations. Doctor Holland I will be on that. Good luck, everyone. I hope we can move quickly."

***

Cassie picked up where she left off with the audio file, pressing the earpiece against her head to block out noise around her. The pirates had been charging deep into the station, hunting down their attackers. Zahl grudgingly followed behind, unwilling to be left alone but just as concerned about what his crew might find.

***

Zahl's crew progressed through the modules the captain led them through earlier. They heard screams ahead. Men and women crying out, chanting some sort of gibberish. It seemed to echo through the walls, coming from all directions. The chilling sound only intensified the further along they went.

Near the heart of the station, doors opened to the right and left. Men charged in, rapid firing their weapons. Even their wild aim managed to get lucky, taking two men down in an instant. Zahl threw himself backward, slamming into the door as he lifted his own weapon to retaliate.

The other pirates went wild, some of them throwing their weapons to the ground, others using their rifles as clubs. They went utterly savage, beating their opponents until they were little more than pulp. When it was all said and done, Zahl counted twenty-six of his compatriots still alive, each covered in blood.

Zahl didn't even have an opportunity to use his gun. He never had a clear line of fire throughout the engagement and now that it ended, the pirates looked like savages. They continued on their warpath, heading toward a white light through the next door. As they went, they began to chant, uttering the same gibberish as the foes they'd just killed.

"Um . . . hey . . ." Zahl trembled when he said the words, especially when one of his friends turned to look at him with wild, frenzied eyes. He swallowed hard, electing to remain quiet as they marched, heading into what had to be the very center of the station, one of the larger modules.

A massive globe occupied the center of the room, surrounded by a metal guardrail. Other individuals stood around it, arms raised in the air as they belted out screams, cries of adoration and exaltation. Total zealots, men, and women who lost their minds utterly as they worshipped the strange device.

The pirates joined them, offering up praise to the object. *Why aren't they fighting with each other?* Zahl saw no reason for it but the real question that terrified him, the thing he didn't want to voice, even to himself, was why he hadn't succumbed to the same madness as his crew.

What makes me special? Zahl turned to the object in the center of the room. *And what exactly is that?* It felt familiar like he should recognize it from something but he struggled to think . . . to consider his past before boarding the station. *Something's happening. Only not like these poor bastards.*

Zahl directed his attention up. A black, nebulous void seemed to shimmer near the ceiling, tiny electrical bolts sparked in every direction. It filled him with dread, causing a film of cold sweat to cover his entire body. Mad fear threatened to overwhelm him but he mastered it. An idea came to him, one of total desperation.

I have to get back to the ship. One way or another, I'll find a way to launch it. When I get back to civilization, I'll sell the thing and never take to space again. Zahl backed toward the door, slipping into the hallway. The others didn't seem to pay any attention, ignoring him . . . at least for a time.

Zahl just reached the outer door when all the faces turned to him. They pointed, advancing slowly at first but they picked up the pace. Reaction took him. Zahl opened up with the rifle, tearing through several of them until he spent the magazine. He turned, running through the next station module while reloading his weapon.

***

Cassie leaned back, turning it off. Zahl made it clear he was going to die. His former crew must've found him. Heat discovered all that remained of the man. A splash of blood and his recording device. Her imagination ran wild as to what they might've done to him and she had to shake it off, forcing herself to consider something else.

Vincent touched her shoulder, making her jump. "Hey, it's just me . . . whoa. You're pale. What happened? Are you okay?"

Cassie shook her head. "I . . . guess. Yes. I'm fine." She drew a deep breath. "The Orb is there. In the middle of the station. It's . . . guarded . . . by . . . by maniacs."

"You'll have to explain that," Desmond replied.

"Wild people," Cassie said. "Affected by . . . this anomaly we're talking about. They're completely insane. Driven mad by it and preserved to draw energy from them." She sighed. "And it's probably happening to our people over there too."

"We can counter the vibrations," Salina added, "but I'm not sure how well it will work so close to the source. Around it, maybe but right on top? I can't say for sure."

"Try anyway," Desmond said. "I want those men back on the ship as soon as possible. Out of that influence. Good work, Cassie. I wish you would've had better news but at least we know. Keep pushing, folks. Lives are counting on what we do next. Make it count."

Chapter 9

Heat considered the roster of their second team. They were brand new to the Gnosis, but seasoned marines. He hadn't met any of them prior to when they boarded the ship. Most were eager, like Hendricks and Stellen. Each of them wanted to be there, to visit the unknown and defend humanity.

Their first time out, they suffered some kind of strange situation that might've ended them. Heat wanted answers and their prisoner might have them. The man wore the tattered remains of a Pahxin tech uniform. Sleeves were gone, pants were shredded and his cheeks were sliced open from just below the eyes to his jaw.

Blood covered him and not all of it was his own. They secured his hands in front of him. Vine held him in place while Gillet used some smelling salts to wake him up. The man jolted and immediately started struggling. Heat pressed his weapon against the man's forehead but it didn't slow him down, didn't even seem to catch his attention.

"That's not normal," Vine said. "He doesn't even care that you're holding a gun to him."

"He probably knows we won't murder him," Gillet replied.

"Listen up!" Heat barked, using all the command authority he could muster. "I know you think death doesn't matter, that it doesn't scare you but it should. Because we don't have to do it quick. We could make this take a while, just like your buddies in there with their knives and clubs. So answer my questions! What the hell is going on?"

"Gunny," Bosh said. "Door's secure but people are banging on it."

"Understood," Heat replied. He nudged the prisoner. "You still here? Answer me! What's going on? What's wrong with you people?"

The man began to foam at the mouth, jostling about from a sudden seizure. "Christ!" Gillet leaned in and gave him an injection. It slowed him down until he passed out, falling into a deep, sedated sleep. "Did you guys see that? He was moving around like . . . like he didn't care what happened to his bones."

"Why'd you knock him out?" Heat asked. He advanced on Gillet, clenching his fists. "I was questioning him, man."

"Heat." Gillet hesitated, letting out a sigh. "He was having a fit. He couldn't talk anyway. What was I supposed to do? Watch him spasm until he broke his back? His neck? Is that what you were after?"

"I wanted answers."

"You weren't going to get them," Gillet said. "Not from this guy. And I'm pretty sure you know that."

Heat fumed, fighting back a wash of frustrated rage. Intellectually, he knew what was happening. He'd seen it in their opponents but he still struggled against it, wanted desperately to put his fist into Gillet's face. Such feelings never came over him toward a fellow soldier, not with so much honest violence.

He paced away, forcing himself to think through it. As his agitation threatened him, it became more obvious in the men around him as well. *Am I the only thing holding these guys together?* The thought concerned him but made sense, in relation to his time with the Orb. *If that's the case, then I have to keep a firm grip on my emotions*.

Taking several deep breaths, he felt himself calm and the body language of the men around him adjusted accordingly. *Wow. That's incredible*. People still banged at the doors, trying to get in. Heat closed his eyes, thinking through the moment. *Our best path forward is to finish the mission*. ↘

They got their hands on the Orb, they might even save the other people on board. Removing it from the base may just be the ticket . . . and he knew that was true somehow. In the back of his mind, it sounded correct. Unfortunately, it wouldn't be as simple as walking in and taking it.

The opposition would throw their lives away to stop them. He hadn't seen such horde mentality before in all his career as a soldier. Their opponents seemed to believe they had an unlimited supply, that sheer numbers might prevail over superior firepower. The only problems they truly faced were the Tol'An . . . and potentially team two.

He didn't want to think about that but it wouldn't be denied as a terrible possibility.

"They've got cutting torches!" Vine shouted. "They're cutting through the door!"

Heat lifted his weapon, aiming at the door. "Open it up then . . . and step aside." Gillet stood beside him, preparing himself for the rush. The other marines did the same.

Sparks exploded from the bottom of the door but abruptly vanished as Vine opened it up. A surprised, wild eyed man looked up. He wasn't even wearing eye protection, his face covered in tiny burns. Before he could do more than gasp, Heat loaded him up, three shots to the head.

The body collapsed in a pool of blood. Enemies trampled the corpse, charging in with their melee weapons. The marines tore through them, blasting each one long before they could get within range. All told, they finished off seventeen combatants before they stopped coming.

Bosh cheered. "That's right, you freaks! Get some of that!"

Something buzzed, a beam weapon from the other room. The blast caught Bosh in the back of the head, knocking him off balance and to the floor. "Contact!" Vine called, returning fire. A series of beam weapons went off. The marines took cover on either side of the door while taking shots back as they could.

"We can go around!" Gillet shouted. "Take the other door!"

Heat noted Anderson checking on Bosh. "How is he? Did he make it?"

"Life signs are nil," Anderson said. "I think . . . Gah!" Two beams interrupted him, each connecting with the small of his back. He went down, his armor completely melted where he'd been hit.

Vine started toward him but Kelly stopped him, dragging him back toward the wall.

"Damn it." Heat stepped out, firing a rocket into the next module where their attackers were held up. The ordnance hissed as it plunged into the room, exploding when it hit the wall. The door suddenly slammed shut as hair began to rush out from a hull breach. "Whoa! I did not expect that much damage!"

"Really?" Gillet shook his head. "A rocket in a space station wouldn't open the wall?"

"Saved the day, didn't it?" Heat moved over to check Anderson but he was gone as well. Both he and Bosh were dead. Vine crouched by the bodies, head bowed. "Hey . . ." He put his hand on Vine's shoulder. "We have to go, man. I know how it feels, believe me but it's time to preserve the rest of the lives in the unit."

Vine nodded, rising to his feet. They were down to Gillet, Kelly, Brock, Vine, and Erskin. Six men from ten. "We'll come back for them when we're ready to take off. Come on. We'll go through this module over here. Oddly enough . . . I know the best way to get where we need to be."

"Should we be worried about that?" Gillet asked.

"Yes, probably." Heat shrugged. "But at least it's something. I'll take point."

***

Cassie tapped Salina, gesturing to her screen. "Look at this. Do you see that power surge? That's the thing creating the vibrations you're trying to counter and . . . I cross-checked how it happened. Every bump coincides with a life sign winking out. A death. The fighting over there is making it more powerful."

Salina frowned. "I thought this thing wanted people alive."

"The seconds leading up to death might be like . . . an energy drink to it." Cassie pinched the bridge of her nose. "Meaning it would be better to keep them alive but not entirely necessary, you see what I mean?"

"I do . . . So ceasing hostilities wouldn't necessarily help."

Cassie shook her head. "It will continue to feed on them normally *but* from what the pirate's log said, it drives them to violence. It pushes them to hurt each other. Which is ultimately why it lures other ships here."

"More fuel." Salina tapped her com, bringing Doctor Holland on the line. "Do you have anything?"

"I'm working with Chief Webber on a device that *should* cancel out those vibration waves but it's taking more time than we'd like. It needs an incredible amount of power. We're trying to regulate that so it won't just burn out within seconds. I'll let you know when we have something."

Salina cursed under her breath. "There you have it. Everything takes too much time."

Scanners started lighting up. Cassie and Salina both turned to their stations. A large ship emerged from hyperspace, closing swiftly with the station. "Captain!" Salina shouted, far more passionate than Cassie had ever heard her be before. "We have a Tol'An vessel entering the system, on intercept with the station."

"Because why not?" Desmond asked. He got on the com. "All hands to battle stations." He turned it off. "Zach, get the weapons going and move in to engage. We don't need to add more fuel to the fire on that station."

"Sir?" Vincent asked. "Wouldn't it help if they docked? We could take them out from there."

"Two problems with that," Desmond said. "First, we'd have a solid chance at taking the station out. Second, have you been listening to Salina and Cassie? More people would only feed whatever that thing is over there. The last thing we need is to make it more powerful. It could get to the point that it impacts us as well."

Vincent cleared his throat. "Understood. I'll get Raptor out there to help with fighters."

"Good call, get the rest of the pilots ready for round two." Desmond turned to Cassie. "If you've got any sort of stunning plan for getting the Orb and our people back, now's the time to pull it off. Give me a report on our newcomer. What's he like?"

"Destroyer," Salina said. "According to the Pahxin database, they can carry two dozen fighters. Crew of thirty, likely number of soldiers . . . anywhere from twenty to fifty depending on their tolerance for overloading."

"Probably high," Vincent muttered. "Considering who we're talking about."

"Won't matter when this is over." Desmond leaned back in his chair. "Hail them, Salina. Let's see if they feel like talking."

Cassie ran a scan over the vessel herself while Salina attempted to reach the Tol'An ship. They hadn't raised their shields yet but were heading straight for the space station, moving at an alarming speed. It didn't seem like they would stop, nor even slow down. Did they intend to ram it?

Fighters deployed a moment later, ten in all. They raced in the direction of the Gnosis, forming up as they went. Their armaments appeared to be on par with others of their class, beams and regular shields. Something did stand out, a single missile on each. High yield explosives, which might've been capable of damaging the Gnosis if the shields were down. Shuttles launched next, each one full of soldiers. They rocketed toward the station, three in all. Scans indicated they loaded up with eight men in each. Twenty-four troops hoping to secure the Orb. Considering what was happening there, their chances of success were incredibly low.

"They've warned us off," Salina said. "Recommended we leave the system immediately or we'll be destroyed."

"Lock weapons," Desmond said. "Zach, you can fire when we're in range."

"Captain," Cassie moved over to his chair, "they may be as blind as we were when we first arrived."

"Meaning?" Desmond asked.

"That they don't know about the boneyard or the fact that they're sending their soldiers into a station full of psychotic people doing God knows what."

"Ah . . ." Desmond rubbed his chin. "Interesting point. How dense is that debris field?"

"Bad," Salina said. "A large ship could not make it through there unscathed. Some of the larger pieces of rock alone are bigger than the Gnosis. Not to mention the fact that we're dealing with some pretty hefty pieces of ship. A few are mostly intact with terrible hull breaches. Probably what killed their crews."

"But there is an upper side to it, correct?" Desmond turned to look at Salina.

"Yes, sir . . . I don't follow the point?"

"Just this." Desmond gestured to the screen. "If we lure the enemy ship close enough, we might get them to crash into it by trying to pursue us."

"How would we get them to follow?" Vincent asked. "They have no reason to bother with us if we don't try to stop them from boarding the station."

"We disable their shuttles with our fighters," Desmond replied, "and while that happens, we move to the field. I'm thinking you folks are good enough to deceive their scanners. Make them think we already have the Orb. Then, initiate a fake hyperdrive jump. Should get their attention."

"I'll get on it right now," Salina said. "Shouldn't be too difficult to make that happen."

"Zach, get us into position." Desmond smirked at Cassie. "You might need to help Salina. Vincent, give the pilots their new mission. Stopping those shuttles is key. If they get aboard, they'll detect the Orb is there. As long as they shoot those down, the Tol'An destroyer shouldn't last more than a few minutes."

***

Dennis led the fighters back toward the Gnosis, ready to board for the remainder of the mission. After being told to withdraw from the station, he figured they were done. When the enemy ship emerged from hyperspace, he groaned internally. That meant sane pilots, people with some self-preservation.

Fighters appeared on their screens first then moments later, three shuttles. Raptor emerged from the Gnosis, racing out to join them. *At least we'll have overwhelming odds,* Dennis thought. *Now to make that matter.*

"Dennis," Vincent's voice came through the com, "You guys need address those shuttles. They cannot be allowed to board the station. At all costs, those three *must* be disabled. Do you read me?"

"Understood, sir." Dennis checked his scan. "We'll have to haul ass to get there before they try. What's going on?"

"Captain's got a plan to handle that destroyer. Get to it. We'll be keeping an eye out from here."

"Listen up, folks. New mission." Dennis let them know their objective. "Anna, take your Charger squadron up against the pilots. Dimitri, back her up. Mustang will deal with the shuttles. Any questions before we dive in?"

"Why the hell is he giving orders?" Flying Officer Carson Bright, Raptor Five asked the question. "Seems to me he has no right to be telling us what to do. He's not my direct commander."

"Stow it," Squadron Leader Dimitri Gerrit ran Raptor. "You know better than to be like that. Dennis has operational command. Follow our lead. We're going after those ships. Now be quiet."

"I don't like it," Carson insisted. "Screw that guy!"

"Consider yourself on report," Dimitri said. "Fall in line, now Raptor Five! I won't give you the order again."

Dennis didn't know Carson well but he'd never had problems with the man before. The fact he popped off didn't seem much like him at all. *What the hell is he thinking? I'll have him brought up on insubordination charges! Bastard.* Rage formed in his gut, spreading frustration until he felt on the verge of losing control.

"We're all on the same side here," Alicia said. "Save your attitude for the enemy, huh?"

"Shut the hell up, Quinn," Carson barked. "No one asked you."

"Dude . . ." Alicia lowered her voice. "You want to go a round, asshole?"

"Enough!" Anna stepped in. "Bickering at a time like this? You're all on report! Focus on the fighters. Dennis, I'll get our people where they need to be. Go for the shuttles. We have limited time before all of this is pointless. Come on." She engaged her afterburners, flying straight for the enemy ships.

Commentary ended but Dennis nursed his anger, still half tempted to turn on Carson and blast him a couple of times.

That thought finally dragged him out of the moment. Even considering an attack on a fellow flyer fell so far outside his normal paradigm, it broke through the rage and anger, casting it aside. *That didn't feel remotely natural*. He checked his scanner. They'd be on the enemy shuttles inside two minutes at maximum speed.

Not enough time to investigate what just happened.

When Alicia threatened Carson, that hadn't been enough to push Dennis out of his anger. Ultimately, it didn't matter. He directed his ire toward the Tol'An shuttles, focusing on them. They could not be allowed to take the station, to board or dock. He engaged his beam weapons, sending a quick message to his team to focus all firepower on the nearest vessel.

Turrets popped out from the tops of the shuttles, firing blasts in their direction. Dennis dropped down to make it harder for them to target him. He depressed his trigger, tearing into the enemy's shields. The other ships of Mustang did the same, ripping through the enemy defenses in one run.

As they spun around, Dennis had them switch to guns and they blew the shuttle out of the sky. In the back of his mind, he recalled the order to *disable* the shuttles. Did the Gnosis intend for them to take prisoners? That didn't seem likely given the severity of the situation, of what they needed to do.

The next two shuttles attempted to fly evasively, moving erratically. Several of his people hammered the ship with missiles before following up with guns. Mustang Four, Lieutenant Kate Zeller, several direct hits from the turret as they came in for the kill. Her shields winked out and the enemy attack tore through her cockpit, causing the entire ship to go up.

"Kate!" Dennis shouted. He knew she didn't eject, saw clearly that her ship had been obliterated. Within a matter of seconds, there was nothing left. She'd been killed.

He turned his attention the shuttle in question. Its shields were down. He deployed a missile, watching it cut the distance between them in a few seconds before connecting with its target. The resulting explosion opened the back, sending the bodies of soldiers streaming out into space just as the rest of the vessel blew.

One left. "Tear that son of a bitch apart!" Dennis barely recognized his own voice, couldn't believe what he was hearing. He'd never sounded so intense, so savage before. It frightened him, not only of himself but what pushed him so far. They'd lost pilots before. He never lost himself as a result.

Yet the other pilots under his command seemed to do the same. They unleashed hell on that final shuttle, hitting it with everything they had. The shuttle's turret was torn off by a spray of gunfire, then holes appeared on either side from two strafing runs by Mustang pilots. Bits of debris flew off in various directions.

The coup de grace came as Flying Officer Roman Mallard cut through the hull with beams, ripping the top open all the way to the cockpit. That made the ship tumble and it crashed into the station, shattering into thousands of pieces which drifted toward the boneyard nearby.

Dennis's blood continued to boil. He wanted more and there were pilots out there fighting with Anna and the others. He didn't care if Mustang went with him, half hoped they wouldn't bother. Altering course, he headed toward the action, kicking his afterburners to full. His people formed up with him.

Apparently, they wanted another piece of the Tol'An as well. He couldn't blame them. When they finished at the station, they'd go to their base and wipe them clean from the universe. Everyone would be better off after their execution, after their total extermination. Dennis fully intended to be there, to witness their end.

Terrorists deserved extinction. Humanity would be the ones to give it to them.

***

Dulain's com unit lit up while he sat in the operations center. Christina reached out on his private channel. He stepped out of the room, ensuring he was totally alone before he accepted the transmission.

"I didn't expect to hear from you like this," he said. "Is everything in order? I'm in private . . . relative private."

"I've got a lot of data to go through," Christina said. "We're going to need to be sequestered with it. I'm hoping for a room with a shower attached so we can get cleaned up and go to work. Maybe one of the long-term apartments? Stock it up with food. We might be a while."

"I'd hoped for more immediate intel," Dulain said. "What do you have that I can feed the admiral? Or some of his cronies?"

"Not much," Christina said. "The facility was fully occupied by some force. They weren't wearing insignias . . . Maybe mercenaries or part of this terrorist cell. We downloaded info from their terminal though so I'll know who they are soon enough."

"Were you injured?"

"It went loud," Christina replied, "but we're not hurt. Not really. We're going to be back at the base in less than thirty minutes. Can you get the space ready? We'll need a trustworthy escort too. God knows if we have a traitor inside Gamma Alpha, they might make a go at us. In fact, we might even want to clear the tarmac."

Dulain hummed. "You're starting to sound as paranoid as me."

"I learned from you," Christina said, "so I don't think that's a big surprise."

"Cute." Dulain chuckled. "Anyway, I'll have everything ready for your arrival, including some guards. We'll talk after you've settled in. Thank you, for your efforts. Sounds like you had a bit of a rough time."

"To put it lightly," Christina replied. "Christina out."

The line went dead and Dulain hurried back into operation control. He put a few of his agents on the task of finding a good room for the investigation and put things in motion. A few hours later, they would likely have the information they needed to retaliate against the traitors and their people.

When that mission proved to be a success, the AIA would have once again shown their value. Once the military took down the terrorists once and for all, it would likely be the leg up Dulain needed for another promotion. He'd be in the position he wanted, moving into the political arena finally.

But first, the preservation of Earth. Then . . . leadership into the stars. One step at a time.

Chapter 10

Heat blasted an enemy charging him from the left, grabbing the body as it nearly collapsed on him. Had it not been for his armor, he would've been taken to the ground but the enhanced strength afforded by the hydraulics allowed him to toss it to the side. The corpse slammed into the wall with enough force to crack the spine.

Another two jumped on Gillet's back. They were ripped free by Vine and slammed into the ground, their hips and legs liquefied by the contact. Eight more combatants threw themselves into the meat grinder against the marines, trying to hamper their progress. Each enemy body ended up broken on the floor.

They progressed to the next module, drawing ever nearer to their prize. Heat knew they were two away. He instinctually dropped to the ground, half a second before gunfire—their type of weapons—blasted the wall where his head had been a moment before. He didn't rise immediately, remaining behind the cover of a computer console.

"Friendly fire!" Vine shouted. "Stop!"

The guns went off again.

"What the hell are you doing?" Kelly yelled. "Guys, it's us! Stop shooting!"

Heat looked back just as Brock took a full burst to the chest and head. His armor prevented most of the damage but a hose broke free, spraying hydraulic fluid from a seam in his armor. Someone would've had to know precisely where to shoot to make that happen. So if team two had fallen under the sway of the station, they maintained some peace of mind.

The marines standing opposite them on the other side of the room barely resembled team two anymore. They were covered in blood, bits of flesh and clothing clung to their armor. One had a head stuck to the top of his helmet, another carried an arm in his left hand, wielding his rifle in the right.

They'd been busy with the scavengers, likely tearing them apart with their bare hands. Heat assumed this because they hadn't heard gunfire but those men had clearly been through quite a lot. Whatever savagery overtook them manifested in a horrifying way and if they could be saved, any memory of their actions would taint them for life.

"Stand down!" Heat barked. "That's an order!"

"Go to hell!" The screaming voice barely sounded human, let alone as any distinct person. It gave Heat the chills, making him ill to think about one of his people being totally consumed the same way as the others. Yet, this person sounded normal compared to the freaks they'd been fighting.

Perhaps it was a matter of how long they spent on the station as opposed. More exposure might've meant less control.

"I don't think I heard you, soldier!" Heat shouted, once again trying to break through the conditioning. "You will stand down this instant and help us take the objective! Each of you scum sucking piles of shit joined the marines! You are not allowed to succumb to alien intellects! You are the best Earth has to offer! Prove it!"

"We're . . . firing . . . at our own people!" He recognized that voice. Private Conti. He stood out as a poster child marine. Six-three, black hair, blue eyes . . . Looked like a real warrior. If he was coming around, that meant the truly committed men might be salvageable. "Fight it guys! We can't do this!"

The next sound of pure, inarticulate rage came from the man who told them to go to hell moments before. He fired wildly. Conti screamed. More gunfire went off. A massive battle broke out not twelve feet away. Heat directed his people to follow him, to stay low and crawl to the next door.

Heat tapped the panel, moving into the next hallway. Rockets started flying and he cursed. "Move it! All of you get your asses out of there!"

The marines rushed toward the next module just as the hull was torn open at multiple points around the room. The ceiling, floor, and one wall had holes large enough for three men to fit shoulder to shoulder. Air poured through the hole, dragging anything loose into space. Two armored men burst outside, gone in an instant.

Heat stood at the end of the hallway, clinging to the wall. Vine and Kelly crawled inside, turning to the others. They shouted over the coms, telling them to hurry. Brock's damaged armor hampered him and he struggled to crawl toward them. Erskin headed out there to help but not even five feet from their comrade, Brock lost his grip and slipped out of the station.

"No!" Erskin shouted, grabbing the wall and dragging himself back toward the others.

"Come on!" Vine shouted. "Move your ass, Erskin!"

Other marines went flying out, bodies of the fallen members of team two. They were scorched and burned from the rocket attacks, pieces of armor broken free. Heat's shoulders slumped when he saw Conti's body follow them but not all of them were accounted for. Some must've escaped, must've slipped into a different module.

Great, Heat thought, *more targets as well armed as we are*.

Erskin drew close enough for Vine and Kelly to drag him into the hall. They shut the door, ending vacuum. Five of them were left and it was impossible to know how many additional soldiers they faced before they'd reach their objective. Heat knew how close they were but it almost didn't matter.

What would happen when they got there? Even if they got the Orb, how would they get it away? Trying to transport the thing through the station with God knows how many enemies running around sounded like a nightmare. An impossibility if he was to be honest. And that was *if* the other shuttle remained attached to the station.

Without communications, they were isolated, unable to call for help. Moving forward felt irresponsible. *We're throwing our lives away.*

Heat shook his head violently and it suddenly cleared. "Holy shit . . ." he muttered.

"What's that, boss?" Vine asked. "Are we moving out?"

"We should press on," Gillet said. "There's no point in sitting around here right now."

"I just . . . had a moment." Heat looked them over. "Were you . . . worried a moment ago?"

Erskin laughed. "I've been worried since we boarded this bitch." His comment made the others chuckle, though it seemed forced.

"I'm serious," Heat replied. "Did you feel a sense of despair? Something like that?"

"I thought it was because of poor Brock," Gillet said. "Because of team two."

"Partially," Heat said. "But I think it's me."

"You?" Vine shrugged. "What's that even mean?"

"It's hard to explain." Heat sighed. "Let's just be glad I made that trip into the Orb or we'd all be dead right now." He motioned. "Follow me, guys. The Orb is just on the other side of this module. God knows we're about to encounter more soldiers but hopefully, we won't find anymore with weapons like ours. Not for a while at least."

"Someone survived on team two," Gillet said. "Is that what you're saying?"

"Yeah." Heat nodded. "And there are only a few places I think they'd go. The most logical is they've been called back to the center of the station to defend the Orb . . . to keep us from taking it. I think whatever we're facing, the real enemy, knows that it can't *truly* affect us. We've got a small advantage in that way . . . but it makes us prime targets."

"What're we waiting for?" Vine asked, advancing ahead of everyone. "I'm taking point. I want to see whatever this sack of shit is in person . . . and then I'm going to put my boot so far up its ass, it'll be coughing up toe jam."

Colorful, Heat thought. *I wonder if I should tell them that it's not a human being at all . . . that it's some kind of amorphous* thing *without a physical form.* He shook his head. *I don't think they're interested in that kind of bad news just now. We've got enough problems without putting monsters in the equation.*

***

Desmond glared at his personal screen, watching as the final shuttle went down. Robbing the Tol'An of the ability to board the station allowed the Gnosis to initiate their plan. As they closed in on the debris field, he quickly plotted the distance between them and the destroyer.

In less than three minutes, the boneyard would be directly between them and the destroyer.

"Salina, start broadcasting that signal," Desmond said. "It'll take them a moment to realize what they're seeing. Zach, start the energy build up in the hyperdrive. The combination of those two things should be like a beacon in the night. If they don't catch on, they shouldn't be out here at all."

"Yes, sir." Salina tapped something hard. "We're now broadcasting a signal equivalent to the Orb and a touch stronger, just enough to get past any sort of interference the field might present."

"Hyperdrive is online," Zach said. "Ten minutes until our fake jump is ready to go."

"Sounds good." Desmond turned to Vincent. "Are our fighters engaging theirs?"

"Yes, sir," Vincent replied. "And Mustang's on the way to help. They have odds so it shouldn't be too much of a fight, to be honest." He paused. "As I think of it, the Tol'An must've thought the same way we did. There wouldn't be any opposition out here."

"Looks like we all made some mistakes," Desmond said. "Theirs will be fatal." He checked their course again. They were nearly in position. "Has the destroyer responded to the signals?"

"Not yet," Salina said. "They are holding position."

Vincent hummed. "Maybe they know we've never left fighters behind? They might think this is a ruse."

"I guess we'll have to see," Desmond replied. "My experience suggests that the type of opponent we're up against believes everyone plays from the same book. They'd abandon people in a heartbeat if they secured their objective. Why wouldn't we?" He shrugged. "If they call our bluff, we'll deal with it then but at least they can't field troops."

"They are firing up their engines," Salina said. "They're hailing us."

"Really?" Desmond smirked. "Give me audio over here." He waited for the connection to pop in his ear. "This is Captain Bradford."

"Surrender your vessel immediately," came the reply. "This is Montag Zhin of the Tol'An and we demand you heave to for boarding."

"I'm afraid we can't do that," Desmond said. "After all, we've got what we came for. You can have the rest."

"Do not make us fire upon you!" Montag shouted. "Heave to! Now! We are on approach and will be there quickly!"

"By all means then," Desmond said. "Come on over. We'll just power down and wait for your approach." He killed the connection. "Stop the hyperdrive build up. Keep the Orb power going." He turned to Vincent. "This is going to work. I can't believe this anomaly is going to make this possible."

"We're lucky we didn't run into it when we arrived," Vincent said. "Hell, so are they. Now . . . Well . . . We'll see whether a Tol'An destroyer can survive a collision in space."

"My money's on no." Desmond gestured to Zach. "Get our weapons ready, low power to avoid detection. If they make it through, I want to hit them with everything. Finish the thing off before it gets too close. If their reactor goes up, that could cause some damage so we want to keep them away."

"When they go up, the debris will be cast all over this system," Vincent pointed out. "Some of it toward us."

"Good point." Desmond nodded. "Get ready for some evasive flying, Zach . . . and if we don't have to shoot the Tol'an, we'll take care of the largest obstacles." He turned back to his screen, watching as the destroyer closed on them. They were less than five thousand kilometers from entering the boneyard and did not appear to be slowing at all.

They're going to hit that thing at full speed, Desmond shook his head. *That will leave a mark. Hopefully, we've bought our men on the station a little more time. If they're still alive. After we contend with our visitors, I have to find a way to get them out of there. One problem at a time though. One problem at a time.*

***

Anna took a full barrage of energy blasts to the bottom of her ship, flipping as an alarm went off. The attack dropped her shields to forty percent, which showed a marked improvement over the previous designs. During their first engagement, she would've had to eject. Now, she escaped destruction and maintained her defenses for a little longer.

It was still luck though, Anna thought. *That could've been a lot worse.* She marked her attacker, a particularly wily opponent who swung around, trying to get another firing solution. They started the dance, a real dogfight that involved quick passes and short bursts. Now that she was aware of him, he struggled to get her back in his sights.

"We're having a rough time over here!" Lieutenant Preston Everest shouted out. He was acting second in command of Charger, awaiting the word on his full transfer to the position. "Carson's gone crazy!"

When Anna received the message at first, she thought her people were struggling with the enemy. Hearing it involved Carson enraged her far beyond even being shot by the enemy. *What the hell is wrong with that guy?* Her target made a mistake, climbing in front of her for a brief moment.

Two beam shots took down his shields, the third knocked out one of his two thrusters. Thus hampered, his speed suffered and she switched to guns, depressing the trigger until the computer warned her that the weapons were overheating. Letting up, the ship in front of her drifted, half the tail shorn off by the attack.

"So what the hell is going on?" Anna spun around and raced back toward her comrades. The Tol'An vessels appeared to be on retreat but Carson's ship was attacking one of their own. Flight Lieutenant Dylan Ball, Raptor Two and technically, his superior officer. Com net was lit up with people yelling at him to stand down.

Mustang approached, Dennis reached out to Anna for an update. She barely knew what to say. "Carson's gone mad," she finally replied. "He's attacking Dylan and won't respond to hails. We're . . . We have to disable him. Knock his shields out and put him down so we can get him back to the ship."

While she knew that was the right thing to say, deep inside she wanted to finish him off, blow his vessel out of the sky. His insubordination earlier should've been a death sentence. He deserved it, did everything in his power to put himself in a criminal position. Hatred welled up in her stomach and she armed her missiles.

"Whoa, Anna!" Dennis shouted at her. "Those are *not* going to disable his ship! Stand down on those."

"Shut up," Anna grumbled. "There's no reason to let this asshole live. I was wrong. We put him down and show the others that insubordination won't be tolerated in wartime."

"That's not the way to do this," Dennis insisted. "Stand down, Squadron Leader. That's a direct order. I have operational control over this mission and I'm *ordering* you to back off immediately!"

Anna struggled with his command, part of her pushing to obey but the rage . . . The passion demanded action. *I can't do this.* She had a firing solution. It might've hit Dylan but that felt like an acceptable loss to take care of a traitor. And yet, Dennis's order hung in her mind, clinging to her senses and forcing her to fight the urge to kill.

I . . . won't . . . Anna veered off, cursing violently as she did so. The other members of Raptor blasted Carson with beam weapons, whittling away his shields. She turned to watch as they did their best to knock him down carefully. He finally joined them on the communications channel.

"You'll all burn in hell for this!" Carson shouted. "Traitors! Each of you! I can't believe you'd do this to me! To the cause! Humanity is doomed!"

"Stand down," Dimitri barked back. "Disable your weapons and surrender your vessel, Carson! We're taking you back to the ship to get you some help."

"I won't succumb to your criminal behavior!" Carson screamed inarticulately for a moment, as if in agony. "No! You cannot take me! I refuse to be! This is the end! Die! All of you die!"

A power surge erupted from his vessel. Raptor ships burst away from him, hitting their afterburners as his core went critical. Anna's eyes widened. *He's initiated self-destruct! What the hell happened to that man?* But inside, she knew that he'd been possessed by the same hatred and anger she had felt moments before.

Only he hadn't been able to fight it off. The fighters gave him distance as his ship exploded. Carson did not eject. A bright light consumed his vessel and when it faded, he was gone.

"Jesus Christ . . ." Dennis whispered over the com but his voice still sounded loud after the moment of silence. "Team, I want everyone back onboard the Gnosis immediately. That's an order."

"What about the other fighters?" Alicia asked. "They're getting away."

"Going back to their own ship," Dennis replied. "I don't want a repeat of what we just saw with Carson. Return to base *now*. I won't repeat that order."

Anna heard a little of the rage in his voice, a bit of the anger that nearly drove her to fire a missile at her ally. She complied, sending the same message to her unit, reinforcing the need. They formed up and flew back, a solemn bunch after what they'd just witnessed. *If this happened to us, what has happened to the marines?*

The thought made Anna sick to her stomach and she felt for them. They didn't have the benefit of simply leaving the area, of returning to base to get some help and avoid further contact. She couldn't imagine what they might be seeing, how bad it might've gotten. She went against her nature when she armed that missile.

How far off could the marines have been? They were a rough and tumble crew, trained to be violent. If those tendencies were enhanced, pushed over the edge, then they might very well be so far gone, they'd never come back. Carson had been an easy going individual prior to that mission.

Hopefully, they had the willpower to fight back. Without it, the space station might be a total wash . . . and the Gnosis may have lost every single ground troop they sent over there. The tragic waste made Anna angry again and she had to fight hard to push it back down. *Now's not the time for extreme emotions. We need to stay calm if we're going to get out of this.*

A task far easier said than done.

***

General Trall sat on the bridge of the flagship, staring at his tablet. They were still in hyperspace but not for much longer. Still, just before they left the Tol'An home base, he received an update as to the whereabouts of Gizan and what might have happened to him on his last mission.

Spies indicated neither the humans nor the Pahxin had his body. Tol'An operatives searched the entire base and all the mining shafts to no avail. While none of that worked out, one of his more clever technical officers located some solid information in a security feed leaving the planet.

Gizan survived and slipped off planet with a group of workers who survived the carnage.

You clever bastard, Trall thought. *What exactly do you think you'll get up to out there? How far can you possibly run?*

Gizan may have failed in two missions but that did not make him an easy mark to track. His skills as an assassin were legendary, even before the Tol'An came into power. Did the man merely want to escape? Or did he have another nefarious plan in mind? He must've known Ezria would execute him for failing again.

This meant Gizan might want to kill Ezria before such a thing could happen.

And he knows the location of our home world. Trall scowled, fighting back a sense of frustration.

Ezria created the problem with his heavy-handed punishment system. Trall understood the need to discipline failure but by putting a man like Gizan on guard, they endangered the entire operation. If he turned to the Pahxin, if he gave them the coordinates to their primary base, the Tol'An could not withstand the force launched at them.

All the Master had to do was give him an option, Trall thought. *If Gizan didn't know for a fact his life was forfeit, he may have come back on his own.*

Worse, anyone Trall sent after the man may very well die trying to apprehend him. He was not only a loose end but a dangerous one capable of more damage than anyone else in the Tol'An camp. *How exactly am I going to handle you, Gizan? Perhaps I can appeal to your obligation, the oath you took to the Tol'An.*

If, through some miracle, he could talk to the man. But finding the assassin and communicating with him would be one of the biggest challenges of Trall's career. Partially because he was not an investigator but also due to the nature of Gizan's skills. If he didn't want to be found, he likely wouldn't be.

There were too many options, too many places he could go. That slip up with the security camera may not have even been an accident. There was a slim possibility that he did it to challenge the Tol'An. *Come find me*, it suggested. *I'll make you pay for wasting your time while I work my way up the ranks*.

"I hope you're not against us now," Trall muttered, leaning back in his chair.

The battleship would be emerging from hyperspace soon, along with his fleet of four destroyers. He couldn't risk leaving the base undefended but he would've liked to bring more. Depending on what he found, he may well have to turn around and immediately leave. Either way, he prepared himself for the immediate threat.

All while the long-term concern of Gizan hovered in the back of his mind.

Chapter 11

Vincent wore a grim expression while reading the report of Carson's behavior in the field, up to his suicide. He related the information to Desmond, keeping his voice low. The anomaly out there caused a man to take his own life. Holland and Salina needed to get that vibration under control . . . for the sake of the marines.

"Salina," Vincent turned to her. "Can you initiate the cancellation of the vibration yet?"

"Wait," Desmond said. "We can't do it yet."

"Sir?" Vincent's brows lifted. "The Marines . . . "

"We're canceling it out in a large area," Desmond explained. "That means we'd be showing the Tol'An the field before they crashed into it. Once they're so far committed they can't pull back, then you can initiate it. Another few moments won't make any difference as far as what's going on at the station."

"And we'll finally be able to board," Gil said, "to see what's happened . . . initiate a rescue mission."

Desmond nodded. "Vincent, get with Fielding and Gabriel about sending in some reinforcements. A couple people should cover it. If it's too crazy, they'll just leave and we'll figure something else out."

"Yes, sir." Vincent tapped the com, hailing Captain Gabriel. He answered right away. "We need to talk about a scouting party. We're about to cancel out whatever's causing people to lose their minds but once we do, we need to check on the people there. Do you have two or three that you can spare in power armor?"

"Fielding and I will go personally," Gabriel said.

"I thought Fielding was still on light duty."

"You try to get him to stick around with all of his men over there," Gabriel replied. "We'll get ready now."

The line went dead and Vincent turned to Desmond. "They're on it."

"Good." Desmond gestured to the screen. "Here they come."

The Tol'An vessel picked up speed, flying straight for them. They would enter the debris field at any moment. Smaller bits of metal and rock hung in space, tapping their shields, not big enough to warrant notice but then, they struck a particularly large chunk of a starship, something big enough to make their defenses flare up.

Salina announced, "they've hailed us, stating we were ordered to stand down."

"Let them know we didn't fire," Desmond said, "though I doubt it's going to matter in a moment."

The Tol'An's momentum carried them further into the boneyard, chunks of debris battering their hull. Their shields lasted through the first several collisions but they dropped abruptly as a particularly massive rock battered them on the starboard side. Fire erupted from hull breaches.

"Excellent," Desmond said. "That worked far better than I could've hoped. Zach, open fire."

Vincent turned to him, "sir?"

"Yes?"

"I think they're already done . . . Do we need to . . . well . . ."

"They're a hostile force," Desmond replied. "They ordered us to stand down so they could take the Orb. Yes, that's necessary. Zach?"

"Captain," Salina jumped in. "Their core is going critical. We should withdraw from the field to avoid damage."

"As soon as we hasten these bastards on their way to hell," Desmond said.

"Initiate the device," Vincent ordered. "Salina, cancel out that vibration. Now."

Salina returned to her post and tapped the terminal several times. A high-pitched whine filled the bridge. Vincent slapped his hands over his ears until it subsided but even when the sound faded away, his skin itched and crawled. Desmond leaned forward, gripping his head for several long moments.

All eyes remained on him before he finally leaned back and drew a deep breath. "Withdraw from the area," he muttered. "Hurry, Zach."

The pilot initiated the maneuver moments before the Tol'An ship exploded. Scanners showed the debris flying in all directions, thrown by the blast. Much of it hammered the space station, riddling it with thousands of chunks of various sizes. If the facility hadn't been so large, the bombardment might've been enough to destroy it utterly.

Automatic defenses blasted some of the larger pieces but it was clear they'd need some help. Luckily, their pilots remained outside and Vincent directed them to sweep the area, cleaning up the larger chunks that threatened the ship. Even so, they needed to remain vigilant until they could leave the area entirely.

"Captain . . ." Vincent turned to him. "You were . . ."

"Yeah, pissed," Desmond said. "Totally enraged by the Tol'An to the point I could barely think. It was incredible."

"The effects of the vibrations," Salina said. "They are far more intense on the station. We've toned them down but not entirely. Those under the effects *might* be calmed somewhat . . . perhaps even enough to be jarred back into a state of control. Depending on what they've done and what they remember though . . ."

"It could be bad," Cassie added. "Imagine realizing you'd committed murder . . . or worse."

"Can we get through with the coms yet?" Desmond asked. "To the station?"

"Trying again," Salina said. "Give me a few minutes."

Vincent shivered from the odd sensation clawing at his skin. The irritation felt far better than the low level of emotional turmoil he'd been dealing with earlier but only just. It might even be enough to drive some of the people on the station crazier, depending on how agitated they already were.

"No signal yet," Salina said. "But the interference has cleared somewhat. I'll set up an automated message to ping them constantly. When they respond, we'll know."

"Good." Desmond scratched the back of his neck. "I want to get out of here as quickly as possible. For the sake of everyone."

***

Heat followed Vine closely through the next module, half surprised to find the section empty. They approached the door to the central chamber, the dead center of the entire facility. As they reached for the panel to open up, a high-pitched whine filled the station, a bizarre noise that his helmet immediately dampened.

"What the hell was that?" Gillet asked. "Did you guys hear it?"

"Of course we did," Kelly grumbled. "God! My skin! It's like shit's crawling all over me!"

"Calm down," Heat said. He felt it too but he forced himself to relax. "Just breathe. We're about to go into the most dangerous part of this station. It could be insane, guys so you have to remain focused. Everyone in this room is going home, right? Every one of you should have that firmly planted in your minds."

They each huffed out a *hoo-yah*. "Good," Heat continued. "I'm going to open the door. Get to the sides in case someone starts shooting right away."

The marines separated, preparing themselves for the coming action. Heat hit the button, sending the door up into the ceiling. He paused, giving Vine and the others a chance to fire but none of them moved. Gillet lowered his weapon. The others exchanged glances, each seemed frozen to the spot.

Heat peeked into the room, taking two steps back. The Orb sat in the center of the room, resting on a pedestal surrounded by something jagged. A closer look revealed bones, dismembered body parts, skulls and other less obvious piles of goo. Men stood around it all in a circle, their arms raised in the air.

Over the Orb, a black cloud shifted and churned with tiny blue bolts of electricity dancing about it. Heat *felt* a presence within that amorphous thing, a consciousness of incredible intensity. It reached out to him, whispering in his ear but that wasn't the whole story behind it.

No, the sound he heard, the words tickling his mind were not from the cloud but his own mind. It tried to trick him by bolstering negative thoughts. He shook his head emphatically, battling it off but it required a serious struggle. The others behind him were dumbfounded by their discovery, protected but paralyzed.

Something made his skin crawl, a sudden tickle covering his whole body. He desperately needed to scratch, wishing he wasn't wearing his armor. While the physical discomfort continued, the mental assault from the strange anomaly eased up. His men advanced.

"Do you feel that?" Gillet asked. "Holy shit, it's like someone's poured ants in my armor."

"At least you can think," Heat said. "Mostly. Look." He directed their attention to the men inside the room. They lowered their arms, scratching at them wildly. Each of them looked confused until they noticed the altar they were surrounding, the horror before them. "They're about to have a bad moment."

"What?" Gillet lifted his weapon. "Shit, they're about to freak out, aren't they?"

Heat nodded, taking aim as well. "Something's hampering the anomaly but it's only doing a partial job. We might not have much time before they become violent."

"Let's get the Orb and get out then," Vine said.

"Won't be that easy . . ."

A door on the other side of the altar room opened. An armored marine stepped inside, instantly opening fire on the idolaters. Bodies hit the ground, none of them reacted swiftly enough to survive the onslaught. Gillet took aim. "Shit, Heat! What do we do with this? What do we do?"

The marine cut down the last of them, turning his attention to the Orb. He began to lift his weapon. Heat shouted, "light him up!"

The whole team blasted away and Heat prayed they had the type of aim they should've given their status. Their target took most of the hits, dancing backward toward the door. His armor gave him an edge over the others and he dashed through the door. There was no way he walked away unscathed. Adrenaline must've carried him out.

"Secure this room!" Heat shouted. "Gillet, you're with me. The rest of you are in here. Anything comes in besides us, you kill it. Let's go!"

Heat dashed through the room with Gillet close behind. They burst into the next hallway, each dodging to the side as their opponent fired at the door. They shot back, driving the man further away from the Orb, toward the sound of approaching footsteps. Dozens of them, perhaps more of the pirates or Tol'An, it was impossible to tell.

Before they reached the next room, they heard their former companion's weapon fire again. He began to scream but it was drowned out beneath the shouts of others. Heat opened the door, swallowing hard as he witnessed a savage display of horrific murder.

A crowd descended upon the armored marine, ripping his armor off with wild adrenalized rage. In moments, they were at his bare skin, tearing at him until his cries ended. Heat barely had time to think about pointing his gun at them before they'd killed him. One looked in their direction, wild eyes above a blood caked mouth.

"They're *eating* people . . ." Heat muttered. He pulled out a grenade. "Gillet."

His companion did the same. They cooked them both then tossed in the explosives. The door closed a moment before they exploded. Organic splatters filled the air followed by the pained cries of the dying.

"Do you think it's over?" Gillet asked. "Did we win?"

"I kind of doubt it," Heat said. "But if there are more, we have to the Orb away from the anomaly. I think . . . and I don't know how I know this but . . . it's like life support for that thing. It feeds on people but survives because of the power of the Orb."

"And you know this?"

Heat nodded. "Maybe the Orb is the reason it exists . . . It doesn't matter. Come on. I have an idea of what to do."

"What?"

"You won't like it," Heat replied. "We have to get a hold of the Gnosis. I intend to pop a hole in the hull, get the Orb out and let them pull a search and rescue on it . . . and us."

"Wait . . . Us?" Gillet followed him as they started walking. "Are you saying we're going to jettison ourselves into space?"

"Safer than sticking around here to see if there are more freaks ready to kill us." Heat patted him on the shoulder. "Come on, every marine wants to take a walk in space, don't they? We've got the jump jets for some minor maneuverability. It'll be fine. What could go wrong?"

"Pretty much everything," Gillet said. "Like . . . if we screw up, the Orb will be trashed on its way out the damn hole."

"Believe me, if there's anything we know how to do well, it's blowing holes in stuff." Heat cleared his throat. "I hope."

"Not filling me with confidence."

"We're coming through!" Heat shouted. "Don't shoot!"

They entered the room and found their companions standing still, staring up at the anomaly. "Crap . . ." Heat muttered. "I hope I can bring them back."

"Yeah, how do you do that again?"

Heat shrugged. "My presence was what kept you guys okay before."

"It's not helping now."

"Give it a minute." Heat tapped his helmet, bringing up the com. "Gnosis, this is Gunnery Sergeant Heathrow. Do you copy?"

***

Fielding suited up, wincing as the armor clamped down over his bad shoulder. It had healed fairly well but wasn't all the way there yet. Doctors said another five days without strain. How many would it take after his excursion to the station? That was anyone's guess. Providing they stuck to the plan of checking the situation and leaving, they should be fine.

He met Captain Gabriel in the hangar. The older man looked terribly severe wearing the suit, his cropped gray hair tight against his tan scalp. Fielding never understood how Gabriel maintained the skin tone when they spent so much time at space and he didn't want to ask. If the man used a spray, it would be disappointing.

"You up for this?" Gabriel asked. "No real shame if you say no."

"Sir," Fielding tilted his head, "are you seriously asking me that?"

"Had to. Conscience wouldn't let me go without giving you a chance to back out." Gabriel shrugged. "Glad to know I was right about you . . . Even if it is a bad idea."

They boarded the shuttle, Gabriel shut the door behind them. The pilot worked on getting clearance for them while they strapped in. Once the shuttle cleared the bay doors, Fielding peered out at the station, frowning at all the visible damage. It had been through hell and most of it seemed to happen after the Gnosis arrived.

"Sir," Fielding said, "what do you make the chances of them still being alive on that thing?"

"Slim," Gabriel replied. "If I'm to be honest. That place is pretty hosed. It would be a miracle if anyone's alive. I think we're heading over there to confirm a lot of deaths . . . and possibly recover the cargo we came for."

"No room for hope then, huh?"

Gabriel shrugged. "I've run a lot of ops on both sides of the com. There's always room I suppose . . . and Heathrow's pulled off some impossible nonsense. I can't put anything past that guy."

Fielding smirked at that. They had seen him do some crazy things. He deserved a promotion and when things were side and done, he'd very likely get one. If he survived. It really was difficult to think of him as lying dead on the desolate station, after all he'd been through and done.

But he felt the same way about Sergeant Gorman. That man's record spoke for itself and he sacrificed himself for the greater good of his team. The number of good men humanity lost in their skirmish war took quite the toll. Many who thought they were simply going into space to explore the galaxy were gone.

Can't be these guys, Fielding thought. *They're too stubborn to die*.

"We're five hundred kilometers to target," the pilot said. "Picking up life signs on board. Interference is making it hard to tell just how many."

Of course it is. Fielding rolled his eyes. This time, the problem probably stemmed from the destruction of the Tol'An ship nearby. That explosion left a tremendous amount of radiation. Some of the fighters had to clear the area around the Gnosis to make it safe to board. "Docking will be a challenge, at least on this side of things."

Gabriel peered out the window. "The highest concentration of life forms seems to be near the center. We should probably swing around and get as close to that as possible."

They stared around the structure, pulling further away from the Gnosis. Fielding kept a sharp eye on his own scanner, checking for enemy fighters. They were all supposed to be destroyed, but with all the scanner problems, there was no way to know for sure. Anything could be hiding out there.

Something pinged his com, a signal coming from nearby. Fielding tried to acknowledge it but it was already gone. *Damn it!* He tapped at his wrist computer, revealing it from the armor to try and trace the source but it had happened too fast. He half thought he might've imagined it.

"Did you get a signal just now?" Fielding asked. Gabriel began to answer when it happened again. "Sorry, sir. Hold on." It became stronger as they drew closer to the center of the station. "I've almost got this. It could be a message from the team . . . or at least someone . . . on board the facility."

"Gnosis!" Heat's voice came through garbled and messy, but it was clearly him. "This is . . . Can you . . . me?"

"Heat?" Fielding shouted. "Can you hear me? Hello?"

"Lieutenant!" Heat's voice came through much better, still garbled but more distinct. "You have no idea how good it is to hear your voice. Thank God!"

"Are you okay? Where are you? We're in a shuttle on our way to the facility. We can pick you up."

"That's good news," Heat said, "but not for the reason you think. Don't bother to dock here. We're about to leave."

Fielding frowned. "Leave? How? Where? What're you talking about?"

"Um . . . well . . . we have the Orb but getting it out of here is going to be a challenge so we thought we might jettison it . . . and ourselves." Heat didn't stop there. "If you're already in a shuttle, we can hook up that way. It makes this plan slightly less crazy . . . and gives it the potential to work."

"I see." Fielding sighed. "One second."

"Begging your pardon, sir, but we don't have much time."

Fielding shook his head, quickly explaining the plan to Gabriel. The captain chuckled in response. "Of course he came up with something like that." He turned. "We're going to need to head down. I'll inform the Gnosis we just turned this into a rescue operation. Fielding, do your best to coordinate with those marines and let's bring them home."

"Okay, Heat," Fielding said, "we're moving into position to support you. Get it done . . . as safely as this crazy plan will let you."

"Will do, sir." Heat's connection fizzled out as another rush of interference cut them off.

"Gabriel finished giving the news to the ship, laughing again. "Those boys sure know how to make an exit, huh?"

"You sure we should've enabled them to pull this off?"

That seemed to push Gabriel over the edge and he really cackled. "You think we could've stopped em? Sure, threaten with a report or some other nonsense but you and I have no idea what they saw or had to do over there. We don't even know how many are left. If they have a way to escape, they're going to take it . . . even if it's slim."

"A million things could go wrong," Fielding said. "Suit malfunction, getting torn through a hole too small . . . Those are the two off the top of my head."

"Yeah, true. So just imagine why they're willing to take those risks." Gabriel put his hands behind his head. "That's the kind of improvisational thinking I like to see in marines. I just hope more than two or three of them survived."

A morbid thought, but Fielding understood where it came from. Before they even boarded the shuttle, he resigned himself to writing letters to the families of every man on the station. It would be particularly difficult for the first timers, the guys who had only *just* left the planet.

But it wasn't a complete loss. That was the point to focus on. All the rest, the mourning and anger, could wait.

Chapter 12

Cassie ran a scan over the station again. With the counter in place for the strange vibration, she hoped any masking would be gone. Sure enough, she located the device in the center of the station. A limited number of life forms seemed to be around it but in the outer sections, those that weren't damaged, there were still quite a few people.

She sent a ping to that section of the facility, hoping to get a communication through but there was too much interference from the destroyed Tol'An vessel. Their shuttle seemed to be going around the station then abruptly headed for what would be considered the bottom. Plotting their course showed they were heading for the center module.

"Captain, I've got the Orb," Cassie said. "I've marked it on the schematics of the facility."

"Heat reported in," Desmond replied. "Got through to Lieutenant Fielding. They're going in for a pickup but they haven't explained the plan exactly. It doesn't involve docking though."

"I'll get fighter escort," Vincent added.

Salina sent a message to Cassie, pointing out another reading from the area. An unstable mass . . . Big one. Explosives, probably enough to detach the entire module from the whole. It would likely just pop a hole in the thing. When the Tol'An ship exploded, sending shards into the walls of the facility, it didn't prove to be particularly resilient.

"Who would do that?" Cassie asked. "Surely, this isn't *our* people? They must be trying to destroy the Orb."

Salina shook her head. "You've spent enough time with those marines to know better than that. Come on now. Do you really think they didn't come up with a way to detonate their remaining rockets to get out of there?"

"But the explosion . . ." Cassie shrugged. "Am I wrong that this is endangering the device?"

"Yeah, I'm sure it's endangered." Salina frowned, peering at her screen for a long moment. "They might have a plan. Those men tend to be experts at explosives . . . small arms. I'm sure if bombs are coming out, or whatever they specifically rigged up, then they aren't planning on harming the reason they went there."

Cassie didn't feel quite as sure. She'd seen the marines act recklessly before. Yes, it worked out then but this was something else entirely. The energy stored in the Orb held enough destructive power to turn the station into dust. So far, no one managed to push the limits of their structural integrity.

Looks like now is the time.

"I wish we could get through to them." Cassie tried again with no success. "Damn it!"

"Captain," Salina said. "There's a distinct possibility they plan to blow up that part of the station to *create* an exit. If that's true, there's potential for the Orb to be damaged."

"Get Fielding on the line," Desmond said. "Find out what's going on and see if this is something we need to stop."

"I'm on it."

Cassie hoped they knew what they were doing. One false move could kill every living thing in the immediate vicinity. The Gnosis couldn't move quickly enough to avoid the blast if it went off in the next few minutes, never mind the pilots still out mopping up the drifting bits of boneyard making travel hazardous.

One of the uses the Tol'An had for more than one Orb involved weaponizing the energy. They could drop one in a major city, detonate it and cause catastrophic damage, the likes of which even the Pahxin may have not seen before. Depending on where they spent their device, they held the potential to bring a government to their knees.

But the marines knew the stakes. They heard the briefings and Heat, in particular, understood the capabilities of the ancient technology. If anyone should've respected them, it would be him.

I'm really trying to trust you, Heat, Cassie thought, *but you're not making it easy when you start pulling this kind of thing.*

***

Heat helped place the rockets while Gillet handled their personal, one shot shields. They hadn't used them throughout the engagement but he was convinced he could use them to shield the Orb from the blast. Each of them would undoubtedly be burned out but it would be enough to keep the device whole.

I hope that works or this whole sector goes boom. Heat stepped back as they finished placing twelve of the rockets. "That should be all of them. They're set for remote detonation. Let's get into the hallway, shut the door and blow them from there." He turned to Gillet. "How's it going with those shields?"

"They're almost ready," Gillet said. "I had to put them in key locations over the device to keep it safe." He looked up at the strange cloud. "Doubt it's going to affect that thing though."

"Once the Orb's gone, that thing dies," Heat replied. "Don't look at it." He started to turn away and paused. The computer terminal near the Orb was *live*. Lights flashed over it. *This culture must've been studying the Orb. What is this cloud though? It must've been what finished them off.*

Gillet patted his arm. "Let's go, man. We need to make this happen. Fielding isn't going to wait forever."

"Yeah, I get it." Heat shook his head. "Come on, men! Everyone in the hallway!"

Screams sounded from somewhere else in the station, rapidly approaching. "God damn it!" Vine shouted. "We were too slow!"

"Don't worry about it," Heat said. "Once the bombs go off, no one but us can survive in there. Get ready."

They closed the door and Heat counted them back from three. "Fire in the hole!" He hit the detonator and the station shook violently, making them clasp at the walls to maintain their footing. Lights flickered all around them. Hate filled screams turned to terror, people who had regained just enough of their senses to fear death.

The station began to quake violently. Gillet grabbed Heat's arm. "This whole place might be coming apart, man! We need to get the hell out before the station tries to seal the breach!"

"When we open that door," Heat said. "It's going to suck us through the hole. Be ready. It won't be fun." Just . . . keep your limbs tight to your body and use your thrusters the best you can. Shuttle's out there . . . We gotta get there. You ready for a real ride, marines?"

They gave another *hoo-ah*, though Heat recognized the forced zeal behind it. This might've been the craziest thing he'd ever done so he understood where they were coming from. When we returned to the Gnosis, if they survived, they'd have a real story to tell the folks back home.

Heat braced himself, slinging his weapon. He reached for the panel, tapping the button. The door slid up and he was immediately sucked into the room toward a massive hole in the wall and floor. The Orb was gone along with several of the computer panels. Only the cloud remained, roiling and sparking alone in the ceiling.

He sailed through the room, carried by the suction though there couldn't be much air left. It swept him out into space, tossed well away from the open hole. He tumbled, closing his eyes to avoid becoming ill from the sudden weightlessness. Something bumped him to the right and he opened his eyes, coming in contact with a bloated body.

They surrounded him, dozens at least, all lifeless and still. Some part of his brain suggested he should panic, or be upset about it but he remained steadfast, almost dead inside to the carnage around him. Even as he turned and saw the station modules start to separate, he still felt a profound sense of calm.

I've survived another one, Heat thought. *These odds are getting ridiculous*. He engaged his thrusters, slowing his spin so he regained control of his motion. It took trial and error before he steadied and stopped rotating. It helped settle his stomach, though the vastness around him threatened to overwhelm his senses.

"Christ, that hurt!" Vine shouted. "Thank *God* my armor held!"

"What happened?" Heat asked. He couldn't see the others. "Everyone sound off."

"I whacked my shoulder on the way out," Vine replied. "We all made it . . . though Kelly bounced off the wall on his way."

"It was bad," Kelly said. "I *swore* felt a seal break. Luckily, I was wrong."

"So where the hell is this shuttle, Heat?" Gillet asked. "I'd like to get the hell out of here as quickly as possible."

Heat craned his neck, looking all around for their transport. Off to his right, he saw the glow of the Orb, floating some distance away. At least it stuck out enough to be seen from just about any distance. If the Gnosis needed to do the pickup themselves, they'd be able to. *Mission accomplished, I guess.*

"Lieutenant, this is Heathrow. Please respond."

Two fighters flew by, seemingly less than three hundred yards off. It made Heat's heart race for a moment and he switched his com over to the wide tactical net. "Hey, stop flying in this sector!" He shouted. "Repeat, do *not* fly through this sector. There are people floating out here."

A red light appeared on his HUD, indicating his oxygen reserves had less than ten minutes before they'd be exhausted. *Why the hell not?* "Conserve your oxygen," Heat said. "No unnecessary talking. I'll keep trying to get people on coms." He recorded an automated message and started broadcasting it, working hard to keep his breathing shallow.

I need to buy a little more time. Just another few minutes. Come on, Fielding. I know you're out there.

***

Salina stood suddenly, her scanner lighting up with the explosion on the station. Bodies were cast through the hull, dozens of them spilling through the breach as if they'd been backed up, waiting for the pressure to release. Half a moment later, the Orb burst free as well, drifting into space alongside the corpses.

"Cassie!" Salina gestured to her without looking up. "Check your scan!"

"The Orb!" Cassie turned. "Captain, they released it. It's floating!"

"Gabriel's shuttle is out there," Vincent said. "They'll collect the Orb and whoever made it out of that insanity."

"I'm trying to get them on com," Salina added. "Just give me a moment."

Desmond asked, "how're we doing with debris, Zach?"

"Clearing up," Zach said. "Fighters are helping. The larger pieces, I took care of. Shields are holding against the smaller pieces that aren't worth wasting shots on. I still think we need to pull well away from this area before we start calculating our trip home. Especially with the station seeming to fall apart."

The view screen showed the module separating as the facility finally gave in to all the damage it had received over the past few hours. Salina found it sad, in a way. That place remained intact for some uncountable number of years before they all converged on it and brought it down.

How did it last so long?

"Coms are clearing up," Salina said. "I should have Gabriel on the line in just a moment. I'll help direct them to where they need to go to get the Orb. Looks like we're on mop up duty at this point."

"We'll stay on alert for now," Desmond said. "We still don't know exactly what caused all this chaos in the first place and I'd like some answers before we call everything good. Bring our people onboard so we can wrap up our investigation and get out of here. And I want to know our casualties so far."

Salina nodded. "I'll work with Webber to make sure communications are a priority. We've got pilots holding a perimeter right now around the Orb and I've got Gabriel on the line. They're almost in position and should be pulling the folks in shortly." She paused. "I just got a message from Gunnery Sergeant Heathrow."

"What's it say?" Desmond asked.

"Damn it." Salina sighed. "They're running low on oxygen. I'll try to get them to hurry, sir. Looks like we've got a little less than seven minutes before they run out. For an operation like this . . . it's going to be cutting it close. At least I've got their beacons up. That's something but . . . oh no . . ."

Vincent prompted her when she didn't continue. "What is it?"

"There are only five beacons . . ."

That comment hit like a ton of bricks, temporarily silencing the bridge. The marines had gone over with two teams of ten. To be reduced to so few . . .

Cassie broke the silence, "maybe some of them are still on the station."

"Maybe," Desmond said. "We won't know until they're on board. Move it, people. Those men didn't go through hell to suffocate out there. Look alive. They deserve every chance we can give them."

***

Fielding stood near the back door, waiting for the opportunity to throw it open. He and Gabriel secured themselves with tethers and stood ready to deploy out to help the others aboard. The pilot slowed them down as they approached the Orb. Scans showed the marine beacons were nearby, within six hundred yards from their current location in various directions.

The pilot slowed the ship, bringing it to a halt. A moment later, they had the green light to open up. Fielding dropped the ramp and leaned out, immediately regretting his eagerness. The vastness of space yawned before him, casting severe vertigo over him. He struggled, fighting back nausea just as Gabriel dragged him in.

"Careful there," Gabriel said. "Probably not the place you want to be sick."

"No sir," Fielding replied. "Wow . . . I hadn't anticipated . . ."

"No one does." Gabriel stepped out on the ramp. "We trained for this early on but you got hurt before we did the drills again. Okay. Let's take a look here . . ." He peered at his scanner. "We've got a marine just over there. Pilot, reverse thrusters, roughly two hundred yards."

"Yes, sir." The shuttle began to move, shaking as it did. Fielding held on tight, squinting out the back of the ship as they moved. The first man came into view, slowly tumbling head over heels. Gabriel called for a full stop, grabbed an extra tether and launched himself out the back.

Using thrusters, he maneuvered to the man and secured him, tugging it twice. Fielding hoisted them both back into the shuttle. The process felt like it took forever but couldn't have even been a full minute. When they were back onboard, Fielding attached oxygen to the marine's suit and Gabriel continued the search.

They inched about the area, collecting the men until only one remained. His beacon flashed not far off, near to the Orb. *Two birds, one stone,* Fielding thought. The ship moved toward them as an alarm went off, the countdown for oxygen. "We're out of time," Gabriel said. "Hurry it up, pilot. He could be suffocating already."

Tiny bits of debris hovered around the final marine along with several dead bodies. Fielding noted it was Heat. *Of course, it's him. Why wouldn't he be the last guy?* They needed to be cautious as they approached, nudging the chunks of metal and rock floating about them rather than hitting it with any real force.

Two chunks tapped the wall hard enough to make the whole shuttle shake. Fielding winced, half convinced they'd see a hole appear but the armored hull repelled it. Gabriel launched himself out again, rocketing forward. He reached the end of the line and needed a little more slack.

The shuttle inched back but overcompensated. They zoomed toward the floating soldiers, coming on them much too quickly. "Forward thrust!" Fielding ordered. "You're about to crash into them!"

A quick burst of engines slowed them sufficiently but it was damn close. Gabriel hovered out there at arm's length and they pulled him and Heat into the shuttle. Attaching oxygen to Heat's suit, Fielding ran a quick, diagnostic on his life signs. He was alive, though he'd passed out at some point.

That probably saved his life, Fielding thought. *Took less oxygen.*

"Now to get the Orb," Gabriel said. "We'll wrap it in cargo webbing and drag it back. There's no room in here for it and us." He turned to Fielding. "I'll go out and do the work. You just make sure this is secure. Might take a few minutes. I'll reach out to the Gnosis and tell them what's going on."

"Alright." Fielding got help from the marines as they took down the cargo netting attached to the walls and secured it with multiple tethers. Providing they moved slowly back to the ship, they shouldn't have any trouble. He figured they had all the time they needed. After all, their enemies were defeated.

Something shimmered far off to the left, a strange light some distance away. At first, Fielding thought it might be the sun reflecting off of debris, metal pieces catching the light but then the ships began to appear. They looked like warships, though he wasn't sure of the make or design.

"Are those reinforcements?" Fielding asked. "Pahxin ships?"

Gabriel cursed. "No, son. Those are not. We have to hurry."

"Why? Who are they?"

"Tol'An." Gabriel turned to him. "Get me the net. The Gnosis will be impatient now that they've arrived. I'd give us twenty minutes at most to board the ship and get the hell out of here. Which leaves absolutely no room for error, no mistakes. You gotta love the last-minute challenges, huh?"

"Could've done without it, sir." Fielding handed him the net. "We're ready back here. Good luck."

Chapter 13

"Are you kidding me?" Salina groaned before turning to Desmond. "Sir, you won't believe this but six Tol'An ships just emerged from hyperspace! A battleship and five destroyers to be specific." She checked again. "They haven't moved yet. I'm guessing they're checking up on their friend."

Desmond rubbed his eyes. "Nothing's ever easy." He looked at Vincent. "We can't take them on. That's way too many. How close are we to having our guys back? The Orb?"

"They're getting close." Vincent checked his terminal. "Fielding is reporting to me that they're securing the Orb right now. All marines are accounted for. They've requested medical aid, which is standing by in hangar two. I'd give us another ten minutes, fifteen at the most. We both know they're cutting safety corners."

Desmond nodded. "Salina, let me know when they start moving. At full speed, how long would it take for them to get into firing distance?"

"Twenty minutes, sir," Salina said.

"Five minutes could be the difference between whether we live or die," Desmond said. "I love the odds." He scowled. "Give them the bad news. We need them back fast."

Vincent got on the com and Salina turned to her own station, brows lifting as a hail came in from the enemy battleship. She screened it, noting they were actually seeking a parlay. "Sir . . . the Tol'An want to talk to us. They've opened a channel. It seems you'd be speaking to a General Trall."

"Put him on screen."

Salina complied, turning to see the commander of the enemy. Black hair was cropped short and two prominent scars decorated his left cheek and forehead. Stunning blue eyes peered at them through a hardened expression and he scowled as the connection established, pursing his lips before speaking.

"My name is General Trall of the Tol'An. I demand an explanation for what has happened here and what part you played in the destruction of our people."

Desmond raised his brows. "I'm Captain Bradford, commanding the Gnosis. If you're referring to the destroyer, they seemed to have an unfortunate accident when they plowed into a boneyard. As far as the rest, I'm not sure what happened on the station yet. We're piecing that together ourselves."

"And you had nothing to do with the destruction of that vessel?"

"They did attack us prior to their accident," Desmond replied. "However, I'll tell you what. We are on the verge of leaving. Give us another few moments and you can investigate the sector to your heart's content. We won't stand in your way. Frankly, this place could use your special touch to clean it up."

Trall paused for a moment as he seemed to be listening to someone off screen. When he spoke again, his brow furrowed, making the scar on his forehead look far more sinister. "A Trindisha is floating in space here. We will be claiming it. If your shuttle is attempting to secure it, have them stand down."

"Can't do that," Desmond replied. "But I appreciate your concern. We'll take good care of it."

"We have an overwhelming force," Trall said. "If you resist, we'll destroy your ship."

"Maybe." Desmond leaned forward. "But have you thought about what would happen if we destroyed the device? Just detonated it? The energy stored in that thing holds the potential to vaporize half this system . . . maybe all of it. No one's blown one up before. Would you like to witness it right now?"

"You wouldn't dare." Trall shook his head. "No, that's why you're here. To collect that object. Just as our people were. Stand down, Captain Bradford. This is your last warning."

"If we stand down, can we get some sort of special treatment?" Desmond asked. "Maybe you can ensure we would make it home? Get my people proper medical attention? That sort of thing?"

"This conversation is ended." Trall cut the com.

"Damn." Desmond leaned back. "I hoped I could keep him talking for a while longer. Buy us some time. Is he moving?"

Salina checked her scans. "They have started their engines and are on approach."

"The countdown has started then." Desmond turned to Vincent. "Get those people back on board fast. They do not have any time to dally. Every second will count. Zach, spin us around so we can get out of here. Plot a course for Earth. Salina, help him out. Efficiency isn't as important as getting us out of here shortly after the shuttle arrives."

"We're on it," Zach replied. Salina joined him at his station to work through it. The captain continued speaking behind her.

"Make sure everyone's ready for this. I have a feeling they'll want to strap in for this one. It might get a little rough."

***

Heat felt pressure on both sides of his head like someone was trying to crush his skull in a vice. He woke with a start, struggling against the tether holding him in place before rough hands stopped him from moving. "Settle down!" The words sounded far away but the voice was familiar. "Dude, you're fine. Just relax!"

"Gillet . . .?" Heat asked. "What the hell's going on?"

"We're trying to get the Orb secured to this shuttle so we can escape the incoming Tol'An pricks," Gillet said. "Seems they brought a fleet to back up their buddies."

"Jesus . . ." Heat turned to look outside. Gabriel was moving about the Orb, surrounding it in cargo webbing. "Captain Gabriel's in it? Wow . . . We are in trouble if he's out here."

"We came together," Fielding said. "But he's still got it. Look at him go."

The captain moved with incredible grace, using his thrusters to maneuver about the Orb like a real master. If Heat didn't know better, he would've said the CO had been doing it his whole life. *That's why he's in charge*, he thought. *The man makes everything look pretty damn easy.*

"Can we help?" Heat asked. "Anything we can do?"

"No," Fielding replied. "He just has to finish getting it attached. We're almost done."

Heat turned his attention to the station. Most of the modules had separated, drifting slowly away from the whole but one, in particular, glowed orange in the seams. He focused, really staring at it for a moment before tapping the lieutenant on the arm, directing his attention to it.

"I'm scanning that," Fielding said. He inhaled sharply a moment later. "Um . . . the power core is going critical."

"Damn it." Heat bowed his head.

"What's it matter?" Vine asked. "Let the thing explode."

"If it explodes," Gillet explained, "then those module parts will start moving. It'll create a bigger hazard and it could make things hard for—"

Before he could finish, the reactor blew, scattering the pieces of the engineering module in all directions. The rest of the station, even the parts mostly intact, began to rush away from the center. Two of them moved on a direct course for the shuttle, rapidly growing larger. Heat's eyes widened as he took it in.

"Sir, you have to get back inside," Fielding said. "Captain Gabriel, we have no time. Get back in the shuttle immediately."

"I only have one more tether to link up." Gabriel paused. "Shit. I see what you mean. Go. I'll ride the Orb back to the ship."

"That's crazy, sir. We have to move too swiftly. It's not safe."

"We don't have a choice," Gabriel replied. "I'll try to get this tether linked up while we're moving." He paused. "Pilot, take us back to the ship. Immediately."

"Yes, sir."

The thrusters engaged and the shuttle began to shake as it pulled away from its position. The module seemed to chase them, still closing in for several more moments. Heat swore they'd be hit, even braced himself for the impact. The pursuing piece of debris filled his field of view, blocking out all of space.

They banked to the left, pulling away and out of the object's path. The chunk sailed by them, tumbling off into open space. Chunks seemed to trail in its wake and one of the larger ones struck one of the two tethers securing the Orb to the shuttle. It frayed, remaining intact though only barely.

"Damn it!" Fielding stood, moving out to examine the damage. "It's pretty bad. We're going to lose it. Ideas, gentlemen?"

Gillet stepped forward. "I've got it." He took his own tether off and launched himself out to the Orb. Clinging to the one good line, he attached the line to the cargo net just as Captain Gabriel inched his way around and began back toward the shuttle. "Coming now." He started to crawl back toward the shuttle.

A rock slammed into his shoulder, knocking him to the side. He clung to the line with one hand, dangling in space. "No!" Heat got up and nearly threw himself outside but Fielding stopped him.

"We've got two men out there already, we don't need a third," Fielding said. "Captain, secure Gillet!"

Gabriel was nearly back to the shuttle but turned, using his thrusters to clear the distance. He grabbed Gillet's arm and yanked him close before pulling them both toward the shuttle. When they touched down on the ramp, Fielding attached another tether to Gillet and helped them both back to a seat.

Heat slapped Gillet's arm. "Dude, we had more lines! What were you thinking?"

"That this mission wasn't going to be a waste of men's lives," Gillet replied. "That we weren't going to lose that damn Orb. And . . . I admit . . . that was a little impulsive."

"Stupid," Gabriel said, "but it can be forgiven considering what you've probably seen today." He looked outside, gesturing to the approaching starships. "Look out at the enemy, boys. We're doing this to stop them . . . to prevent space from having the added danger of terrorists threatening your lives."

"Do you think we'll make it before they can attack us?" Vine asked.

"That's on Captain Bradford," Gabriel said. "I'm just here to pound the ground with you fellas. Everything else rests on the shoulders of the flyboys." He sat down. "Estimated time to docking?"

"Five minutes," the pilot said. "Everything secure back there? Seems like we're having a pretty smooth time of it."

Fielding shook his head, speaking up. "Yeah, everything's just great. Total cakewalk back here. Thanks for noticing."

***

Cassie witnessed the sudden reactor meltdown on the station as it cast the modules in all directions. "That did it," she said. "The station blew up. That boneyard just got a whole lot worse . . . and this system has become a real hazard." She mapped the trajectory of the largest pieces and sent them to Zach. "We need to move."

Desmond came to her station and took a look. "It never rains but it blows up, huh?" He turned to Vincent. "Where's that shuttle? Now we've got Tol'An *and* destroyed station to worry about."

"ETA five minutes," Vincent said.

"And our hyperspace coordinates?" Desmond asked.

"We've got a decent course," Zach said. "We're just taking this extra time to optimize a little."

"Good." Desmond sat back down. "How soon before the Tol'An can start shooting?"

"Ten minutes," Cassie replied. "We should have plenty of time to get away."

"Providing nothing else goes wrong," Vincent pointed out. "Don't count on our luck just yet."

"Now's not the time for pessimism," Cassie said. "Please remain positive."

Desmond smirked at the comment. "What she said." He checked his console. "Looks like all stations are reporting ready for the hyperspace jump. Um . . . Cassie, what's going on with that shuttle? Are they *dragging* the Orb?"

She checked her scanner then rubbed her eyes. "Yes, sir. Likely they just didn't have room for the men, their power armor *and* the Orb. Pretty incredible."

Vincent chuckled. "You should just be glad the marines themselves aren't trailing behind it like they're water skiing."

"I guess there is that." Desmond shook his head. "Start the countdown, Zach. Whatever you've got will have to do. Hold on tight, everyone. The second they're confirmed onboard, I want us to jump."

***

Trall stared at the viewscreen, willing the ship to move faster. He saw the surge of their hyperdrive, the power build up indicating they were on the verge of escape. The Trindisha was *just* within his grasp, being dragged out there in space by a lone shuttle with no backup. Yet it all remained outside of reach.

He could not give up, even in light of what might be certain defeat. Any delay might get him the prize. That could be anything from a short in the human's equipment to the sudden destruction of the nearby station causing debris to hit their vessel. Unfortunately, he had the same concern and directed two of the destroyers to screen them.

Come, Captain Bradford. Make a single mistake. I will exploit it.

Scans showed the shuttle rapidly approaching the Gnosis. They would be in a firing solution in mere minutes. The race was on and Trall knew they had no choice but to push. He had engineering open the reactor, forcing it to produce thrust at over a hundred and thirty percent. It bought them a few precious seconds, perhaps enough to hit them with *something*.

Beam weapons were powered up. He ordered his weapon's officer to prepare himself. The shuttle flew into the hangar and along with it, the Orb. Trall ordered his people to fire, to let loose with everything they had. The lights flickered overhead from the strain on the reactor, the guns going off while the engines pulled heavily to maintain their speed.

Time slowed down as the lights from their attack raced toward their target . . . and it winked out of existence, plunging into hyperspace mere moments before the attack would've hit. Trall slumped in his seat, feeling the weight of failure rest solely on his shoulders. They did not manage to catch them, failed to retrieve the Trindisha and lost many men.

If only we would've arrived ten minutes sooner. Trall knew there was no one to blame for their involvement, no one that could take punishment for the loss. Ezria hadn't even told him before sending the destroyer into the unknown. The fact any Tol'An arrived to witness the human victory at all was due to his quick thinking.

"Scan the area for any survivors," Trall said. "See if we can find anyone alive to salvage this mess." He knew the likelihood of saving anyone was next to nothing. The system was a total wreck but he had to try. Understanding how they lost the destroyer and the other ship would give them decent intelligence for the future.

If it ended up mattering. The humans took the final Trindisha, adding it to their collection. The Tol'An might not survive a month, depending on what their enemies chose to do next. But until that time, Trall planned to do his duty and that meant focusing on that moment, finishing his investigation . . . then reporting what happened to Ezria.

The part he looked forward to the absolute least.

***

Vincent let out a cheer as they went into hyperspace and he was joined by Zach. Desmond slumped beside him with relief but he wore a big smile. They saw the attack coming, knew they had but fractions of a second to escape and they did by the skin of their teeth. With their prize.

"Congratulations, everyone," Desmond said. "We've done it. The Orb is ours and the only ones left are in the hands of the Tol'An. This war is one step closer to being over with. Good work."

"Casualty reports coming in." Salina's comment sobered the bridge. "Five marines survived the station . . . We lost one pilot to . . . to suicide."

"I want to know what happened here." Desmond turned to Cassie. "Do you think the information might be with the Orb?"

Cassie hummed. "Possibly. I'll head down and see what I can find out right now."

"Good." Desmond patted Vincent on the arm. "Head down and check on the marines. Make sure they get medical treatment and take their report. We'll meet back up in my office in a couple hours. Zach, what's our ETA for Earth?"

"Six hours," Zach replied, "give or take a half hour. In our hurry, I can't be sure which it'll be."

"That's good enough for me," Desmond replied. "Okay, just a few more things to do before we can get some rest. Again, thank you all for your efforts today. You did fantastic. Get to it and I'll buy you all a free cup of coffee from the cafeteria. Which hopefully will *not* be burned by the time we get to it."

"No promises there," Vincent said as he approached the door. "I love that we have faster than light travel but our mess hall can't seem to get the coffee right."

"Priorities," Cassie replied. They boarded the elevator together. "Maybe when we're done trying to win a war, we can focus on some luxuries."

"It'll be nice to worry about something mundane for a change." Vincent hit the buttons for their two destinations. "And even better to be done with the fighting."

Epilogue

Cassie didn't have to use anything special to interface with the Orb to answer Desmond's question. The basic interface used during the experiment was still in place. She had the technicians move it then she queried the thing like she'd done countless times before joining the Gnosis crew.

As with the others, it proved to be no different in design or architecture. Once she essentially plugged it in, the computer provided the same top-level interface she was accustomed to. It likely contained different information, stored from the previous culture that utilized it, but that didn't hamper her from accessing the data.

Half an hour of searching later, she pieced the story together. The culture used to live on the fourth planet of the system. While their technology advanced rapidly with the discovery of the Orb, they struggled with criminal violence. Many of their population lived beneath their poverty line, unable to make ends meet.

This led to muggings and worse. Those with extreme wealth, less than one percent of that world's population, tasked their scientists to find a solution. They turned to the Orb and developed a device to pacify violent emotions. It followed a similar principle to the culture that copied their minds to computers.

The big difference was that they generated a powerful field they could blanket whole cities with. Something went wrong. Their initial tests seemed fine but a simple tweak and accidental mass deployment sealed their fate. Instead of pacifying the people, that small change pushed them to extreme violence.

The field fed on the Orb, expanding its mindless influence over the entire planet. It caused a violent pilgrimage as millions moved to the facility where the Orb was stored. The goal was to worship it, to pay homage as their minds became consumed with savage violence and a singular goal of possessing the device.

Those few scientists who survived the initial purge and didn't succumb took the Orb into space, bringing it to their high-tech facility. They hoped to save their planet, that by removing the object of the people's desire, they would return to normal. Unfortunately, the anomaly no longer required the Orb to keep it active.

Millions of lives did that and as they escalated the violence, they generated enough power for it to project a version of itself to the Orb. The scientists guessed it wanted to have the object returned but it didn't matter. The beings on the planet surface indulged their madness, eventually destroying the entire planet.

Those few who made it to the station succumbed to the smaller anomaly, killing each other before a final one, much like the pirate Zahl, recorded his thoughts and was slain.

It all started as a means to prevent violence but instead caused it. Cassie finished her report and prepared it for her briefing. *We've learned a lot about people going too far. I hope our people take these lessons and don't make the same mistakes.* She rubbed her eyes as Gil entered the room.

"I see you have finished." Gil sat beside her. "I'm eager to know what happened."

She told him the story, handing him her tablet so he could read some of the entries for himself. He looked down upon it, a deep frown marring his features. "I've seen many dead cultures. Several died by their own hands. The tragedy of such a thing has never gotten easier to take. Once we learn about the end, there is relief . . . then sorrow."

"We have to publish these findings," Cassie said. "Hell, someone needs to write an entire paper on what these different places have done. It will be the only way to avoid our own people going too far."

"Yes, scientists can be overly ambitious," Gil agreed. "I've written some articles on it but they were published by archaeology journals. We need to expand the scope. And we haven't even talked about the fact that this . . . field . . . survived after the people essentially shut down the source of it."

"Technology out of control." Cassie drew a deep breath. "I have to present these findings to the senior officers . . . then I'm going to sleep."

"You look like you could use it." Gil gestured to the Orb. "I think I'll stick around and probe what else we can learn about that culture. There must be some good amongst the tragedy. There's nothing to dig up . . . nothing to collect. The sum total of their entire species is locked up in this Trindisha."

"Which is about the biggest downer I've ever heard." Cassie clapped his shoulder. "I'll leave it to you to preserve their memory. Talk to you later on, Gil. Good luck."

Cassie left, heading for the briefing room. The thought of an entire culture becoming extinct took some time to process but by the time she arrived, it really weighed heavily on her. As they investigated these places, found the Orbs, they found more and more civilizations that reached a peak . . . then toppled.

Humanity only just started up the slope but she worried about how fast they might reach the top . . . and whether or not they would fall down like the others. Those others may have advanced too quickly, gone beyond their cultural ability to absorb change. It might even explain why the Orb on Earth had gateways for them to unlock more knowledge.

Perhaps when each culture died, their Orb sent a final message to the others, building one more layer to pass through before discovering more secrets. That was something Cassie wrote down for later investigation. Probably when the conflict with the Tol'An ended and they could finally direct their attention to the mysteries of the alien technology again.

***

Christina and Essex spent the better part of three hours poring through the data they discovered. Much of it involved the logistics of moving military personnel and equipment about the globe but then, they hit pay dirt. They found the plans for the attack on Gamma Alpha and discovered a base where the vast majority of troops came from in North Africa.

Satellite photos showed an abandoned camp in the mountains but according to the logistics, an underground bunker provided refuge for the troops. They were transported by truck to an airbase then dropped in miles away. Traveling by foot, they got into position and waited for the order to attack.

A man on the inside gave the signal, a human officer in the military. Christina had gone through all the people working there and hadn't uncovered anything. The person was referred to as *Red Corsair*, but beyond that, there was no description. That individual must've been the one who coordinated with the Tol'An, who provided the data.

But that meant an infiltration from the Pahxin to a human. There was another layer of the conspiracy to uncover but they wouldn't find that data in what they stole.

Christina found account information and began a trace. This would lead her to the source of the Earth terrorists and they could arrest the ringleader, then destroy his army. But she was far more concerned with the mole in their facility, the traitor that essentially threatened their way of life.

"Red Corsair," Christina said it out loud, turning to Essex. "We've got a new lead. One that should lead us to the target."

"I thought we were after the armed forces," Essex gestured vaguely outside, "the ones the military wants to hit."

"They'll get their glorious battle," Christina replied. "I want the real traitor. That's the person responsible for all of this. By now, they could be on the Gnosis . . . They could be gone. I need your help with this. You and I are the only ones who know about Red Corsair. We're going to run the bastard to ground."

"Just say the word," Essex said. "What do I do?"

"First, I want a list of everyone that managed to leave the base since the attack. Double check their movements and where they went off to. Compile another list of everyone who hasn't come back. I want to know where they are too. Anyone who has ever worked here at Gamma Alpha and gone to North Africa? I want their names."

"Shouldn't be too many there, right?" Essex asked. "After all, no one goes to Africa for fun these days."

"You're right about that." Christina turned to her computer. "I'll send a report to Dulain about what we've discovered and let him know our investigation is continuing. By tomorrow morning, the military should be ready to plan an operation and we'll be going through the records to find the real target."

"Shouldn't we just wait until we have the ringleader in custody?" Essex shrugged. "Seems like we could save a lot of time if we interrogate him."

"A lot can happen during an apprehension." Christina shook her head. "No, we have to assume he won't talk . . . assume he'll be accidentally shot . . . assume that we're on our own, essentially. Besides, any evidence he provides may not be true. No . . . we'll figure it out ourselves and when we're done, we'll be certain of the results."

"Thank you for bringing me in on this," Essex said. "It sure beats the analytical work I was doing before."

"Don't thank me just yet," Christina replied. "By the time we're done, you might be ready to leave the AIA. Pouring through documents isn't exactly the most thrilling part of the job, but it gets results. Anyway, you better put on a pot of coffee. We're going to be at this for a while and I don't intend to leave until we've got a lead on our colorfully titled friend."

Printed in Great Britain
by Amazon

62187584R00142